"Get out
Lorel sn

Lewis didn't budge. "I didn't expect that sort of welcome."

"I'm amazed you expected any sort of welcome!" Lorel retorted. "But let's get a couple of things straight. I don't want you in here. I don't even want to see you. Got that?"

"Yes, I've got it," he growled. "But why?"

"Why?" she echoed in astonishment. "Last night you waited until I'd had too much to drink, and then you seduced me. I don't like that. And I don't like you. Is that plain enough?"

"Perfectly," replied Lewis, his voice taut and controlled. Then his mouth relaxed a little. "Seduced," he repeated thoughtfully. "That's an old-fashioned word. Are you trying to tell me, Lorel Parker, that you're not a very modern girl?"

JOANNA MANSELL finds writing hard work but very addictive. When she's not bashing away at her typewriter, she's usually got her nose buried in a book. She also loves gardening and daydreaming, two pastimes that go together remarkably well. The ambition of this Essex-born author is to write books that people will enjoy reading.

Books by Joanna Mansell

HARLEQUIN PRESENTS

HARLEQUIN ROMANCE

Don't miss any of our special offers. Write to us at the following address for information on our newest releases.

Harlequin Reader Service
901 Fuhrmann Blvd., P.O. Box 1397, Buffalo, NY 14240
Canadian address: P.O. Box 603,
Fort Erie, Ont. L2A 5X3

JOANNA MANSELL

night with a stranger

Harlequin Books

TORONTO • NEW YORK • LONDON
AMSTERDAM • PARIS • SYDNEY • HAMBURG
STOCKHOLM • ATHENS • TOKYO • MILAN

Harlequin Presents first edition March 1990
ISBN 0-373-11250-5

Original hardcover edition published in 1989
by Mills & Boon Limited

CHAPTER ONE

LOREL trudged on to the platform at Victoria Station, dumped her heavy case with a sigh of relief, and then looked up at the Departure Board. A smile of excitement touched her mouth as she saw it announced the imminent departure of the Orient-Express. And she was going to be on it! All right, so perhaps it had been crazy to spend that legacy from her great-aunt on this horrifically expensive trip instead of something sensible—like some new furniture for her distinctly shabby flat. The last couple of years had been pretty depressing, though, and she had suddenly felt the urge to break out and do something that was a little mad, but *fun*.

Well, this was breaking out with a vengeance, she told herself a trifle ruefully. Blowing several hundred pounds on a train journey that was only going to last twenty-five hours! Too late to change her mind now, though. She just had to go ahead and enjoy every single minute of it.

She picked up her case again, and marched over to the special desk that had been set up on the platform to deal with passengers for the Orient-Express. She checked in, handed over her luggage, and was just turning away again when she felt hard, strong hands gripping her shoulders. Then they whirled her round, almost throwing her off balance.

'So you decided to come after all, you contrary little bitch!' snarled a man's harshly angry voice.

Stunned by the sudden, unprovoked attack, Lorel just gazed dumbly at the tall, tense figure looming over her. She found herself staring straight into a pair of furious vivid blue eyes, which darkened with shock as they raked over her face.

'You're not Melinda,' the man said abruptly. Then, without another word, he wheeled round and quickly strode off.

Now that she was free of that blazingly blue gaze, Lorel began to recover her wits. 'Haven't you ever heard of such a thing as an apology?' she flung after him, but it was too late. He was already out of earshot, and he obviously had no intention of coming back to apologise for his mistake.

Realising that the other people standing around were now staring at her with open curiosity, she flushed slightly, and then began to walk away.

'What a great start to a holiday,' she muttered under her breath. 'Meeting up with a mannerless pig like that!'

She hurried through an archway, and then suddenly stopped, the unpleasant encounter completely forgotten for the moment. There it was—the Orient-Express! Chocolate brown and cream, every inch of it had been polished until it gleamed. It was probably the most luxurious train in the world—and the most famous. And she was going to spend the next twenty-five hours cocooned in its warmth and elegance, as it rattled its way from London to Venice.

She found her seat, and then sat looking out of the window, watching the other passengers boarding the train. There was a varied assortment of people, as she had hoped there would be. There were a fair number wearing furs and designer labels, of course, but there were quite a few others like herself; ordinary people who had splashed out on this trip of a lifetime.

She wondered who would be sitting in the seats opposite and beside her. She hoped they would turn out to be friendly, whoever they were. It would be a pretty dull journey if no one spoke to her.

The rest of the carriage was filling up now, but still the seats around her remained empty. Hardly anyone was left on the platform, and it was getting very near to departure time. Lorel gave a small grimace. It looked as if she might be in for twenty-five hours of her own company!

A few minutes later, the train began to pull out. As it moved out of the station, someone finally flung themself down into the seat opposite her. Lorel glanced up, ready to give a friendly smile to her fellow passenger. Then the smile froze on her face, and she gave a silent groan of disbelief. It was the mannerless pig!

On the platform, she had only seen him for a few brief seconds. Those blue eyes were quite unmistakable, though. Once seen, never forgotten, she told herself grimly. At least, not by her!

She glared furiously at the man, but he didn't take the slightest notice. He wasn't even looking at her. Instead, he was staring out of the window. She had the impression that he was looking for someone, hoping that they might still miraculously turn up, even though the train was now gathering speed and beginning to leave the station behind.

Since he wasn't paying her any attention, Lorel took the opportunity to study his glowering face more closely. The vivid blue eyes were set beneath dark, straight brows, which were at present drawn together in an ill-tempered frown. The flare of his nostrils was a further warning of his black frame of mind, while the hard shape of his mouth was set in an uncompromisingly grim line.

Lorel wasn't daunted, though. Leaning forwards, she tapped him very firmly on the arm, determined that he shouldn't ignore her any longer.

His blue gaze slewed round to rest on her, and she could see that there wasn't the faintest flicker of recognition in those extraordinary eyes of his. She shook her head in amazement. He didn't have the slightest idea who she was. He was so preoccupied that he didn't recognise her as the girl he had grabbed hold of, and treated with such rudeness.

'I believe you owe me an apology,' she told him bluntly.

His face registered blank uninterest. 'I do? I've no idea why you should think that——' Then his eyes narrowed a fraction. 'The girl who looks like Melinda,' he murmured under his breath, almost as if talking to himself.

'I've no idea who Melinda is,' Lorel retorted sharply. 'But I'm certainly the girl you pushed around on the platform. If that's the way you treat women, no wonder this Melinda didn't turn up!' she added, with a snort.

He seemed about to make an irate reply, but was stopped by the appearance of a waiter, bringing round champagne. Lorel glared again at the man opposite her; then she lifted her glass and drank the champagne far too quickly. She could feel it fizzing around inside her, making her feel a little light-headed.

'It's a waste of good champagne, to guzzle it down like a glass of orange juice,' he told her coolly. Then he lifted his own glass, and began to drink at a much more leisurely pace. All the time, though, he was watching her, as if something about her had unexpectedly begun to fascinate him. The longer that unblinking blue gaze was fixed on her, the more uneasy Lorel became. She wished there were some other seat she could move to, but all the other places in the carriage were occupied.

He finished the champagne and put down the empty glass. 'Maybe you're right,' he said, his voice far more relaxed now. 'Perhaps I do owe you an apology.'

'Are you sure it's not too much trouble?' Lorel enquired sarcastically. 'I mean, I wouldn't want you to put yourself out!'

'I've always thought that sarcasm is a particularly unpleasant trait in a woman,' he remarked.

'And *I've* never much liked being pushed around by men,' she threw back at him at once. 'Especially when they happen to be complete strangers!'

To her surprise, he didn't react angrily. Instead, he merely lifted one black eyebrow a fraction. 'Then perhaps we should introduce ourselves. I'm Lewis Elliott.'

His unexpected change of tack left her floundering a little. This man seemed to know exactly how to unsettle her, and she didn't like that.

'And I'm Lorel Parker,' she muttered at last, with some reluctance. Then she couldn't help adding curiously, 'Who's Melinda?'

His gaze briefly darkened. 'That's none of your damned business.'

Lorel immediately bristled. 'I wouldn't say that, not after the way you treated me at the station.'

Lewis Elliott gave an irritable shake of his head. 'Don't blow the whole thing up out of all proportion. You're making it sound as if I threw you to the ground, and then hurled insults at you. It wasn't as bad as that, and you know it.'

'Well—perhaps not,' Lorel conceded grudgingly. 'But you certainly didn't behave like a gentleman,' she added firmly.

His eyes suddenly gleamed. 'Perhaps I'm *not* a gentleman.'

Something in his tone made Lorel's nerves curl. She didn't know what it was, and she decided that she didn't really want to know.

Luckily, the waiter came round again at that point, serving lunch this time. Lorel glanced up in surprise. 'I didn't think we'd be eating so soon.'

'This first stage of the journey, down to Folkestone, only takes an hour and a half,' Lewis informed her, beginning to sound slightly bored now. 'They want to get everyone fed before we're all shunted off the train for the Channel crossing.'

Lorel wished he hadn't mentioned the Channel. It was the one part of the journey she definitely wasn't looking forward to. She looked out of the window, and then wrinkled her nose. Although it was early spring, it looked more like a day in February, with heavy clouds scudding across the sky, and a steadily rising wind.

'I hope the crossing won't be too rough,' she said, a trifle apprehensively.

Lewis Elliott was no longer listening, though. He had opened his briefcase, and was now shuffling through some papers, ignoring the food that had been placed in front of him.

Lorel looked down at her own plate. If the sea was going to be choppy, it might be a good idea not to eat too much. On the other hand, she had been too excited to eat much breakfast, and she was starving. The smoked turkey looked delicious, and the cranberry tartlets looked very appetising. She gave a resigned shrug of her shoulders. It was just too tempting. She picked up her knife and fork, and hungrily began to eat.

When she had finally finished, she sat back and looked at Lewis Elliott, who was still absorbed in the papers he had taken out of his briefcase. She could see columns of figures, and several sets of clipped sheets, that looked like contracts of some kind. From that, she deduced he was going to Italy on business, not for pleasure. Why not fly, then? she wondered idly to herself. It was far quicker. And where did the mysterious Melinda fit into all this? Then she quickly reminded herself that it was really none of her business.

On the other hand, it was difficult not to be just a *little* curious about her fellow traveller. Especially since the two other seats had remained unoccupied, leaving her with no one else to talk to. There must have been a couple of last-minute cancellations. Just her luck, she thought with a grimace. Leaving her with the one man on the train that she would rather not be sharing the next twenty-five hours with.

The waiter came and cleared their table, but Lewis Elliott didn't even look up. Lorel had the feeling that he was going to spend the rest of the journey with his nose buried in those business papers. She wrinkled her nose. She wasn't sure if she was pleased about that or not. It meant that there wouldn't be much opportunity for conversation, but on the other hand she didn't think there was very much more she wanted to say to Lewis Elliott.

She looked out of the window, and saw they were nearing the coast now. Her stomach tightened a little at the thought of the Channel crossing ahead, and she began to wish she hadn't eaten quite so much of that delicious lunch.

A few minutes later, the train pulled into the station and ground to a halt. With obvious reluctance, Lewis gathered together his papers and slid them back into the briefcase. Lorel was just about to ask him what was going to happen next, when a couple of ladies in smart uniforms walked through the carriage, handing out envelopes. Lewis tossed his to one side, but Lorel looked with interest at the one which had been slid discreetly into her hand.

'What's this?' she asked.

'Probably seasickness tablets,' Lewis replied briefly.

'Oh, very funny!' snorted Lorel. 'You've obviously got a very strange sense of humour, as well as a nasty temper.'

She slit open the envelope; then she looked down in surprise as two small tablets rolled out into her hand. Then she took out the neatly printed note inside. It informed her that it was choppy in the Channel, and that although their ferry had stabilisers, she might like to take the enclosed seasickness tablets.

The colour rose in her face. 'I thought you were just being sarcastic,' she mumbled.

'I told you, I don't like sarcasm.'

He was already getting to his feet, and as he headed towards the door Lorel rather hurriedly scrambled after him. She might not like Lewis Elliott very much, but he was obviously an experienced traveller, so she decided it might be a good idea to stick fairly close to him.

She still had the seasickness tablets in her hand. She glanced down at them for a moment, and then shoved them into her pocket. When she was younger, she had always been a good sailor. It was a long time since she had last been on a boat but, with luck, things wouldn't have changed. Anyway, she knew that travel-sickness pills tended to make you feel drowsy, and she didn't want to feel half-asleep for the next few hours.

On board the boat, she found that there was a specially reserved lounge for passengers of the Orient-Express. Tea, coffee and biscuits were being served for anyone who wanted them, but quite a few of the passengers were looking with rather worried faces at the heavy swell of the sea, and not many seemed keen to eat or drink anything.

One of the few exceptions was Lewis. He seemed quite unconcerned about the already noticeable movement of the boat.

'I suppose you've got the sort of stomach that can weather a force-nine gale,' Lorel grumbled.

He gave a brief shrug. 'What do you want me to do? Be seasick just to please you?'

Unaccountably annoyed, Lorel turned away from him. Really, the man wasn't making any effort at all to be pleasant or friendly!

Her head was beginning to ache a little now. It was rather stuffy inside the lounge, and fairly crowded. She moved to a quieter spot near the window, but soon realised that had been a bad mistake. From here, she could see the sombre, heavy swell of the sea, the white-tipped, darkly threatening waves stretching all the way back to the shore, which was now getting further and further away. The boat suddenly seemed a very frail thing, in comparison to the force of all that water, and alarm began to stir inside her.

Lorel swallowed hard. She hadn't expected to enjoy this part of the journey, but she had thought she would be able to get through it without too many problems. There was a rather unpleasant feeling in her stomach that didn't have anything to do with the motion of the boat, though, and her legs were beginning to feel horribly shaky.

'Oh, please, let it be all right,' she muttered under her breath. 'This is a big boat, a safe boat. Nothing can happen.'

The panicky feeling didn't go away, though. Instead, it kept getting steadily worse. A little desperately, she glanced at her watch. Even if the crossing went without incident, they were still going to be on this boat for well over another hour. And, since she couldn't get off, she just had to stick it out, no matter how bad she felt.

She could feel her skin getting clammy and, when she lifted her hand to flick a damp strand of hair back from her face, she found her fingers were fumbling and unsteady. An unpleasant dizziness was sweeping over her, and she took a couple of deep breaths, trying to fight it off, but not very successfully.

Then she felt a hand very firmly grip her arm, and haul her to her feet.

'You need some fresh air,' Lewis Elliott said, without preamble.

'No,' she muttered. 'I don't want to go up on deck. I don't!'

He took absolutely no notice. Instead, he marched her across the lounge and out the door at the far end. A couple of sympathetic glances were thrown her way, but on the whole people took no notice. Too many of them were preoccupied with their own physical symptoms as the boat moved further out into the Channel, hitting still rougher water.

Lorel was vaguely aware that she was going up some steps. She was still trying to tell Lewis Elliott that this wasn't going to do the slightest good, but he wasn't taking any notice. A typically overbearing man, she thought to herself resentfully. Then she gave a small gasp as a gust of fresh air hit her face.

'There's no point in staying cooped up below if you're feeling seasick,' Lewis told her briskly. Then he added a little impatiently, 'If you're a bad sailor, why on earth didn't you take those tablets they handed out on the train?'

Lorel was hanging rather grimly on to his arm by this time, and she had her eyes tightly shut so that she wouldn't have to see the grey, heaving expanse of the sea.

'I'm *not* a bad sailor. And I'm not seasick,' she somehow managed to get out through lips that had gone quite rigid with tension.

'Then what the hell's the matter with you?' demanded Lewis.

'I don't like boats!'

She opened her eyes just a fraction, and saw that he was looking at her with a mixture of irritation and bafflement. Right now, though, she didn't particularly care what kind of expression he was wearing. All she knew was that he was the one firm, solid thing in this shifting, tossing world, and she had no intention of letting go of him. Her fingers dug still harder into his arm, and she didn't even hear his small grunt of pain.

'This may seem like a particularly stupid question,' Lewis remarked. 'But if you don't like boats, what on earth are you doing on this trip? You knew we'd be crossing the Channel. Why not fly, if you hate the sea that much?'

'I thought it would be all right,' she muttered. 'I mean, I knew I wasn't going to enjoy this crossing, but I didn't know it would be this bad. I thought I'd be able to get through it OK. And—and I didn't think the sea would be this rough.'

'It's early April,' he reminded her. 'This time of the year, the water's often rough. Why didn't you wait, and take this trip in summer, when the Channel's usually fairly calm?'

'I needed a holiday *now*,' she said defensively. 'I didn't want to wait a couple more months. And I told you, I thought I'd be all right on the boat. And I was, until I looked out of the window and saw the coast getting further and further away. I just panicked, I couldn't help it. I'm *still* in a panic,' she got out in a quavering voice.

'I know that,' came Lewis's dry reply. 'You're hanging on to my arm so tightly that I'll probably be black and blue by tomorrow.'

'I didn't want to come up here on deck,' she mumbled. 'I tried to tell you that, but you wouldn't listen. I don't want to have to look at the water. I want to go somewhere I can't see it at all, and then stay there until we're safely in port.'

'Come on, then. I'll take you back below.'

'Can't move,' she croaked.

'What?' That hint of impatience was back in his voice again.

'Can't move,' she repeated. And it was true. Her legs were completely frozen. The panic had spread right through her, seizing hold of all her muscles and reducing them to an embarrassing uselessness.

'Heavens, how did I ever get involved in this?' Lewis said in some disbelief.

'You tried to help. But you didn't. You just made things worse.'

'Then next time, remind me to mind my own business,' he said a little grimly. 'And in the meantime, we're going to get back below before we both freeze to death. *Walk*, Lorel!'

She wasn't sure if it was the tone of his voice or the way he had said her name, but which ever it was it seemed to free her from her paralysis. She found her legs would move again, and she hurriedly stumbled back down the stairs, still hanging on to Lewis's arm as if it were some kind of lifeline.

At the bottom of the stairs was a narrow corridor, with several doors leading off it. Lewis opened a couple of the doors, and then finally pulled her through the third. Lorel looked around, feeling slightly better now that she couldn't see the heaving expanse of water that surrounded the boat.

'This is someone's cabin,' she said rather doubtfully. 'We shouldn't be in here.'

'I don't suppose they'll mind too much if we borrow it for a short while.'

There was a small porthole, and Lewis drew the curtain across it. The interior of the cabin was rather dim now, but Lorel didn't mind. Somehow, it felt safer that way.

Lewis pushed her, none too gently, down on to the narrow bed, and then disengaged her clutching fingers from his arm.

'Sorry,' she said as he rubbed his bruised flesh. 'I had to cling on to something, and you just happened to be handy.' She looked around. 'I really don't think we should be in here,' she added rather nervously. 'What if someone comes in and finds us?'

'We'll apologise and leave.' His blue gaze fixed on her. 'The alternative is to go back to the main lounge. Do you want to do that?'

'No,' she said immediately. She was feeling much better now, but she didn't want to face other people just yet. Anyway, the lounge had those large windows. She would be able to see the heavy, rolling waves again——

At the very thought of it, she shuddered. She was sorely tempted to grab hold of Lewis Elliott's arm again—the warm, hard touch of him had been curiously comforting—but she managed to stop herself this time. At the same time, she began to feel highly embarrassed. What an exhibition she had made of herself in front of this stranger! His opinion of her must have reached absolute rock-bottom by now.

'Want to tell me why you're so scared of the sea?' he asked unexpectedly.

'I'm sure you're not really interested,' she answered rather stiffly.

Lewis sighed. 'Are you always like this? Or is it because you're scared that it's so hard to get through to you?'

'I don't know why you're even *trying* to get through to me,' she answered defensively. 'On the train, I got the impression that you thought I was nothing except a nuisance. Now, you're suddenly being friendly and helpful. It's very—well, confusing,' she finished in a low voice.

'You think I've got some ulterior motive?'

She could hear the clear amusement in his voice, and to her annoyance it made her flush.

'I've no idea,' she said coldly. 'I don't know what motivates you. In fact, I don't know anything about you.'

'Nor I about you,' Lewis reminded her. 'But I'm trying to remedy that situation.'

'By prying into my private life?'

A familiar glint of impatience appeared in his blue eyes. 'I simply asked why you're frightened of the sea. Under the circumstances, I don't think that's too impertinent a question.'

'I suppose not,' Lorel conceded reluctantly. She still didn't feel relaxed, though, and the fresh waves of tension didn't seem to have anything to do with her earlier attack of panic. All the same, she supposed she owed him some sort of explanation. 'My parents were drowned a couple of years ago,' she said at last, in a tight voice. 'They went out in a small sailing-boat with a couple of friends and—and none of them came back. Until that happened, I never used to be scared of the sea. I used to enjoy swimming and sailing. After the accident, though, I began to stay well away from the water. There didn't seem any point in deliberately dragging up all the old, sad memories. I didn't think it was a major problem, though. Only a natural re-action, after what had happened. It wasn't until I was actually on this boat that I realised it had developed into a real phobia. By then, it was too late to do anything about it.' She managed a rather feeble smile. 'You can't get off a boat in the middle of the Channel.'

'No, you can't,' Lewis agreed. His tone was rather different from what it had been before, and he was looking at her thoughtfully now. 'You know, there are two things you can do about phobias,' he went on, almost conversationally. 'Give in to them, or face up to them.'

'I definitely intend to give in to this one,' she answered immediately. 'There's no way you're going to get me up on that deck again!'

He gave a brief shrug. 'OK, if you want to be a coward——'

'I do!' she said firmly. She had no intention of letting him provoke her into doing anything foolishly brave.

Lewis's blue gaze fixed on her again. 'I didn't think you were the type to back away from problems.'

She looked back at him steadily. 'Since you don't know me, I don't see how you can possibly guess what type I am.'

He studied her consideringly. 'Perhaps not. But I'm fairly sure of one thing. I think that you're *my* type.'

Lorel blinked, not sure that she had heard him correctly. Or, if she had, that he had really meant what he had said.

'What do you mean by that?' she said slowly, at last.

'Exactly what I said.'

'But you can't have the slightest idea what I'm really like,' she objected. 'We only met a couple of hours ago.'

'I know that I like girls with gold-brown hair and gold-brown eyes.'

Lorel gave a quick snort. 'That's nothing to do with *me*. That's just what I look like.'

'But it's a start,' replied Lewis. 'As to whether it goes any further—we could have a lot of fun finding out,' he suggested lightly.

She knew that she ought to find his suggestion completely outrageous. So, why didn't she? Perhaps it had something to do with those vivid blue eyes of his, she decided shakily. When they were fixed on her so unwaveringly, it was difficult—in fact, almost impossible—to think straight. The man should have been a hypnotist! He could have reduced an entire audience to sheeplike obedience by just staring at them for a few minutes.

His eyes briefly gleamed. 'I think that you're tempted,' he murmured. 'But that you're also a little prudish. There are ways of getting round that, though——'

Casually, he slid his hand over her own, enclosing her fingers within his warm grip. It was an unexpectedly pleasant sensation, and when his thumb tickled her palm she jumped slightly but didn't try to pull her own hand away. When his thumb slid up to the sensitive inner skin of her wrist, though, she decided that enough was enough. This had to stop—and right now!

She tried to release her hand, but discovered that Lewis's grip had been deceptively light. Although his fingers had only seemed to be resting gently on her own, she found she couldn't actually free her hand from his.

Nervously, she cleared her throat. 'Look, this is silly,' she began. 'Someone could walk in at any moment. And anyway, I'm hardly in the mood for these sort of games.'

Lewis merely smiled. 'I could soon persuade you to be in the mood,' he said with total confidence.

Lorel's face instantly darkened. She hated men who were sexually arrogant.

'Oh, I'm sure that you're Mr Wonderful in bed,' she said with heavy and deliberate sarcasm. 'But unfortunately for you, I don't happen to be Miss Free-and-Easy!'

To her amazement, he didn't seem in the least offended. 'I never thought for one moment that you were,' he replied quite calmly. 'As for being Mr Wonderful—perhaps that's taking it a little too far. Although I don't remember having any actual complaints to date.'

'Well, you're about to get your first one,' she retorted. 'I've definitely had enough of this!'

'How can you say that when we've done nothing more than hold hands?' he asked, quite reasonably.

'I know when I want something—and I definitely don't want you!' Lorel snapped angrily.

Lewis remained astonishingly relaxed. She thought she could even see the faint hint of a smile lurking around the corners of his mouth.

'Perhaps you shouldn't make any firm decisions until you've sampled what's on offer,' he suggested smoothly.

She stared at him in disbelief. 'Haven't you been listening to anything I've said? I'm not interested!'

Unperturbed, he let his fingers trace a regretful pattern on the back of her hand. 'Is it because I was rude to you when we first met?' he enquired. 'But I apologised for that.'

'No, you didn't,' she retorted. 'You meant to, but you never actually got around to it.'

'Then I apologise unreservedly,' he said charmingly. 'Am I forgiven?'

She stared at him suspiciously. 'I suppose so,' she finally muttered. What else could she say?

Lewis seemed satisfied with that. He got to his feet, and strolled across to the door. 'Since you don't seem to want to take this any further, perhaps we'd better go.'

Thoroughly relieved by his suggestion, Lorel scrambled to her feet. As far as she was concerned, she couldn't get out of here quickly enough.

When she reached the door, though, Lewis casually swung one arm around her, stopping her from going any further.

'It's no good,' he murmured. 'I can't resist a quick sample, even though I know I'm not going to be allowed any more than that.'

His kiss was swift and hard—and totally delicious. Lorel's head briefly whirled, and for just a moment she found herself actually regretting that she had turned him down so firmly. Then he let go of her again, and gently pushed her out of the cabin.

This time, her legs felt unsteady for an entirely different reason. More perturbed than she liked to admit, she followed him back to the main lounge. Just as they reached the door, though, he stopped and turned to face her.

'We'll be in port in about ten minutes. Will you be all right until then?'

'Fine,' she mumbled. In fact, incredible though it seemed, she had almost forgotten they were on a boat.

Unexpectedly, he grinned. 'There's nothing like a little diversion for taking your mind off your problems, is there?'

Lorel's eyes opened very wide as she realised what he was telling her. 'You mean, you did all that on purpose?' she said incredulously. 'Just to stop me thinking about my phobia?'

His grin broadened. 'Believe me, it wasn't any great hardship. If you're OK, go and sit in the lounge until we get into port. I'll see you later.'

'Where are you going?' she couldn't stop herself from asking.

Lewis's dark eyebrows lifted quizzically. 'To the bar. That kiss has started me thinking a lot of very unsuitable thoughts. I need a drink!'

He quickly walked away from her, and Lorel made her way into the lounge and gratefully sank into a seat. The long train journey from Boulogne to Venice still lay ahead of her, and it looked as if much of it was going to be made in the company of Lewis Elliott. How did she feel about that? She didn't know. One thing seemed certain, though. It was highly unlikely to be boring!

CHAPTER TWO

FOR a variety of reasons, Lorel was very glad to finally get off the boat. The Continental train was waiting for them, and she was welcomed aboard and then shown to her cabin. Her spirits began to rise again as she drank in the luxury of the train; the beautifully polished wooden panelling, the gleaming brass fittings, and elegant Lalique lamps. She forgot about the misery of the channel crossing, even forgot about Lewis Elliott's kiss, as she looked forward to the rest of the journey.

Since her cabin was a single, it was very small, but clever lighting and carefully placed mirrors helped to give the impression that it was much bigger than it actually was. There was a comfortable sofa with thick cushions, and a small mahogany writing-table with a brass lamp. Her suitcase had been placed in the ornate gilt rack above her head, and she shoved her hand-luggage up beside it, and then gave a sigh of satisfaction. This was great! Even better than she had expected it to be.

She felt rather grimy after the ferry crossing. Knowing that there was a small sink concealed somewhere in the cabin, she began turning various knobs, trying to find it. She discovered several cupboards, but no sink. Then she turned one final knob, and found that she had inadvertently opened the door which led into the next cabin!

To her embarrassment, someone was in there. She had just begun to mumble an apology when the man raised his head, and she found herself staring into a very familiar pair of vivid blue eyes.

'Oh, I don't believe this!' she said in annoyance.

Lewis Elliott gave a resigned shrug. 'It looks as though we're destined to spend this journey bumping into each other—one way or the other,' he added, with a sudden gleam.

'I was looking for the sink,' Lorel said with some dignity. 'I must have turned the wrong knob.'

'And found me instead,' Lewis commented, his gaze still suspiciously bright.

'I didn't know you were going to be in the next cabin.'

'I didn't arrange it,' he told her smoothly. 'And the door does lock from your side. You're quite safe.'

Lorel knew perfectly well that he was laughing at her. And why not? she thought with some irritation. So far, he definitely hadn't seen the best side of her. She had been sarcastic to him when they had first met, then a gibbering wreck on the ferry, when she had had that sudden attack of panic. And now she was over-reacting again, just because he turned out to be occupying the cabin next to hers.

On the other hand, did it really matter what this man thought of her? She definitely didn't want to impress or dazzle him. Not that there was any chance of that now, she reminded herself ruefully. She didn't know what his opinion of her was, but she was certain it must be pretty low.

'Have you managed to find the sink yet?' he asked.

'No, I haven't,' she admitted.

He came into her cabin, cleared the top of the small mahogany writing-table, and then lifted it up to reveal a marble sink neatly fitted underneath.

'Thank you,' she said. Her voice came out much stiffer than she had intended. Perhaps it was because he was uncomfortably close. The cabin suddenly seemed far too small to hold the two of them.

She had the disturbing feeling that he knew exactly how much he was disconcerting her. There was a bright glitter in his eyes again as he turned to face her, and an amused smile touched the corners of his mouth, making it look far less hard and *very* sexy. Lorel swallowed audibly, and with an effort dragged her gaze away from his face.

'When you've washed and changed, would you like to join me in the Bar Car, for a drink?' Lewis invited.

'Why?'

Her blunt question seemed to surprise him. 'For all the usual reasons,' he said, after a brief pause. 'Do you want me to list them?'

'I just don't know why you're bothering with me,' she told him, quite truthfully. 'You more or less ignored me on the first part of the journey, and then I was a thorough nuisance on the boat. I thought you'd be trying to avoid me for the rest of the journey, not inviting me to have a drink with you. Or are you just being polite?'

'I rarely do anything out of politeness,' Lewis replied. His gaze rested on her levelly. 'I asked you because you're beginning to interest me. So—is your answer yes or no?'

'Well—yes—I suppose so,' she said hesitantly.

'Then I'll see you later.' He walked back into his own cabin, and as he closed the connecting door he gave her a wicked glance. 'Don't forget to lock it,' he reminded her gently.

Lorel hurriedly obeyed. Then she was annoyed with herself for behaving like the little prude that he had earlier accused her of being.

Her face feeling uncomfortably hot, she ran some cold water and then splashed it over her cheeks until she felt them return to their normal temperature.

'I'm not at all sure I like this man,' she muttered to herself. 'And I wish I wasn't having a drink with him.'

Since she had already accepted his invitation, though, she decided that perhaps she had better try and show him a new image. The old one certainly hadn't been very impressive! She dug her make-up case out of her bag and settled down to repair the ravages of the journey.

'"A little bit of powder and a little bit of paint——"' she quoted wryly, as she brushed bronze eyeshadow on to her lids to bring out the golden-brown of her eyes. In the evening, she would change it to gold, which would make them look positively tawny. Then she generously stroked blusher on to her cheeks. After that Channel crossing, they definitely didn't have much natural colour left in them! A touch of mascara, although her thick, dark lashes hardly needed it, and then some lip-gloss to give her mouth a soft shine. Critically, she surveyed the result. 'Not bad,' she murmured. She ran her fingers through the glossy gold-brown curls which fell almost to her shoulders. There wasn't much she could do with her hair except give it a vigorous brushing, and then shake her head so that the curls tumbled naturally back into place.

What to wear was a problem. She knew that a lot of people on the train would be wearing clothes that reeked of money. When she had decided to take this trip, she had known she couldn't afford anything with an expensive designer label, and so she had stuck with clothes that were basically simple in design, relying on their bright colours to give them impact, and her own well-proportioned body to show them off at their best.

For drinks with Lewis, she picked a dress in vivid emerald green. It was fairly close-fitting and fairly short, and she felt good wearing it, which was the main thing. She had the feeling that she was going to need every ounce of confidence she could get if she was going to cope with Lewis Elliott!

She took one last glance in the mirror, and was quite pleased with the result. With a new bounce in her step, she left her cabin and made her way towards the Bar Car.

She was rather shy about going in on her own, but lifted her head and walked steadily forward, determined to look as cool and sophisticated as the other people already sitting around. It was hard to believe they were on a train. It looked just like the bar in a first-class hotel, with uniformed staff hovering around, exotic flower arrangements, small, tastefully lit alcoves, and at the far end, a grand piano. Lorel blinked. A *piano*? On a train? But she definitely wasn't seeing things. She blinked again, and kept walking, making her way towards Lewis, who was sitting on one of the high stools at the long, polished bar.

His gaze slid appreciatively over her as she seated herself beside him.

'Even nicer than I remembered,' he murmured. 'What would you like to drink?'

'Champagne,' she replied coolly, as if she was used to ordering it every day of her life. After all, this *was* the Orient-Express. She was damned if she was going to order something ordinary.

'Let's sit somewhere a little more private,' suggested Lewis.

Lorel instantly felt a nervous quiver go through her. 'I—er—I like it here,' she said, annoyed to find her voice coming out in a betraying squeak.

'I was only suggesting that we move to one of the alcoves,' Lewis said drily. 'I wasn't planning on dragging you off to a secluded cabin, and locking the door.'

'I wish you wouldn't do that,' she retorted with annoyance.

'Do what? Tease you?' He gave an unexpected grin. 'It's very hard to resist the temptation. You look so delicious when you're angry.' Before she had a chance to answer, he stood up. 'Are you going to risk sitting in a quieter spot with me?' he challenged her.

Lorel got to her feet, wishing that she knew how to get the better of this man. Perhaps it would be easier if he weren't so attractive. No, not attractive, she corrected herself. Downright devastating! The trouble was, he no doubt knew it. Even as he walked over to one of the alcoves, practically every female head in the room turned to look at him, some with a quick glance of appreciation, and others with outright lascivious stares.

She gave a silent sigh as she followed him. She supposed she ought to be congratulating herself on having hooked the most attractive man on the train, instead of complaining all the time. After all, wasn't that the reason she had come on this trip? Hadn't she wanted an adventure, some excitement in her life, after the last couple of depressing years? And if there was a tall, dark, handsome stranger thrown in for good measure she should be *grateful*. More than that, she had better start being nice to him, or he would soon find some other lady to share his champagne.

Rule number one for keeping a man interested— talk about him, and not yourself, she reminded herself with a quirk of her eyebrows. And so, as they sat at a quiet table in the corner and began to sip their champagne, Lorel fixed her huge brown eyes on him and tried to look as if she found him the most fascinating man in the world. It was a technique that had never failed her in the past. Most men loved being the centre of attention.

'About the only thing I know about you is your name,' she said. 'I don't even know what you're doing on this train. Are you going to Italy on holiday?'

'No, on business,' Lewis replied. 'Although I intend to take a few days' break while I'm there. Heaven knows, it's long enough since I had a holiday.'

'What sort of business are you in? she asked. She wasn't particularly interested, but it was one way of keeping the conversation fixed firmly on him.

He paused for a moment, and then said, 'Have you heard of Elliott Communications?'

She shook her head. 'I don't think so.' Then she gave a brief frown. 'Hang on a sec. Wasn't that the company involved in a big takeover recently?'

Lewis nodded. 'We made a successful bid for one of our rivals. We're now one of the biggest companies in the field of electronic communications equipment.'

'Oh—er—congratulations,' she said a little lamely.

His mouth curled up in one corner, in an odd little half-smile. 'You don't sound too impressed.'

'Oh, yes, I am,' she hurriedly assured him. She tried to think of something intelligent to say about communications equipment, but couldn't come up with a single thing, and so instead she said, 'If you're going to Italy on business, wouldn't it have been quicker to have flown? Or did you particularly want to travel on the Orient-Express?'

'One train's very much like another,' Lewis said dismissively. 'This one's a little more comfortable, that's all.'

His blasé attitude irritated her, but she tried not to show it.

'Then what are you doing here?'

'I thought I'd be travelling with—someone else,' he finished, after a moment's hesitation.

Lorel remembered that incident on the platform, when they had first met, and he had snarled at her so angrily.

'Melinda?' she guessed. Then she wrinkled her nose. She supposed she shouldn't have mentioned the absent Melinda. He obviously didn't like talking about her.

To her surprise, though, he didn't react so strongly this time.

'Melinda,' he agreed, in an almost resigned voice.

'Perhaps she got held up at the last moment,' Lorel suggested tactfully. 'You'll probably hear from her when you reach Italy.'

'Who do you think she is?' he enquired, in an unexpectedly amused tone. 'Some girlfriend who stood me up?'

'Well—yes,' she said, a little startled. Then, rather cautiously, 'Isn't she?'

'Melinda's an empty-headed idiot my stepbrother, Felix, has got involved with,' Lewis told her succinctly. 'I've been trying to get her away from him before he ends up completely infatuated with her. I thought I'd managed it this time. I arranged a modelling contract for her with one of the top Italian fashion houses, and threw in this trip for good measure, on the condition that she stays away from him. She agreed to think about it, but since she didn't show up, I suppose she still thinks that Felix is a better bet when it comes to a long-term financial security.' He gave a brief shrug. 'She hasn't got the brains to realise that she's chasing after the wrong brother. If she wants to get her hands on any of the Elliott money, then she should be trying to seduce *me*.'

Lorel inwardly bristled. She had been right; this man was totally arrogant! Trying to arrange other people's lives for them, and crediting them with motives that they probably didn't even have.

'There's one other possibility,' she said indignantly. 'What if they really care about each other?' Ignoring the fact that Lewis's eyebrows had just shot up in patent disbelief, she went on, 'And even if this Melinda is everything you say she is, I still don't see that you've got the right to interfere. Don't you think that everyone should be allowed to make their own mistakes?'

'Not my stepbrother,' he said with complete finality. 'I don't intend to see him tied to some brainless little fortune-hunter.'

'What are you going to do about it?' Lorel wasn't sure that she wanted to know, but somehow she couldn't stop herself from asking the question.

'Keep trying different bribes until I finally find one she can't resist,' Lewis replied a little grimly. 'Perhaps I'll try straight cash next time. Most people respond to money. It's an unpleasant, but basic, fact of life.'

Lorel's gaze had gone quite cold by now. She had set out with the intention of making Lewis Elliott talk about himself, but she had found out rather more than she wanted to know.

'I bet *you're* not married, are you?' she challenged him.

'No, I'm not.' His eyebrows drew together rather sharply. 'Why did you ask that?'

'Oh, don't worry,' she assured him bitingly. 'I'm not interested in you myself. You're not going to have to bribe *me* to stay away from you. I just wanted to know if I'd guessed right about you. After all,' she went on, with the sarcasm that she knew he disliked so much, 'how on earth would you ever be able to choose a wife? I don't see how you could ever be absolutely certain that it was *you* she really wanted, and not all that money you obviously care about so much!'

'Have you quite finished?' he enquired tightly, his blue eyes blazing.

'Oh, yes,' she said, getting to her feet. 'And you can drink the rest of the champagne yourself. As far as I'm concerned, it's gone quite flat!'

And, with that, she turned away from him and made a dignified exit from the Bar Car.

Once back in her cabin, she sat and stared at her reflection ruefully. 'Well, you've certainly blown it,' she murmured to herself. 'The best-looking man on the train—*and* a very eligible bachelor—and you have to go and throw insults in his face. Very clever, Lorel!'

All the same, she didn't regret it. If Lewis Elliott had that sort of attitude towards women—and money—then some other unfortunate female could have the very dubious pleasure of his company on this trip.

She sat and stared out of the window for a while, wondering what she was going to do about dinner this evening. She supposed she could have it here, in her cabin, but she didn't really fancy that. On the other hand, she didn't want to eat alone in the Restaurant Car. The trouble was, she had somehow got so tied up with Lewis Elliott that she hadn't had much of a chance to meet and talk to any of the other passengers. Anyway, most of them seemed to be travelling with friends or family, or had already formed small groups. And that left her very much on her own.

Feeling rather sorry for herself, she took down her case and lifted out the dress she had planned to wear for the evening meal. She had bought it from a shop that specialised in good second-hand clothes, and as soon as she had seen it she had known she would look good in it. The rich black velvet would show up the creamy smoothness of her skin, and the rather old-fashioned style wouldn't look out of place on this particular train. And to brighten up the dress, and bring out the tawny highlights in her eyes and hair, she had bought some gold thread and embroidered a cascade of flowers across one shoulder, like a one-dimensional corsage.

She slid the dress on to a hanger, and then gazed at it regretfully. It looked as if she wasn't even going to get the chance to wear it.

A knock on the door made her jump slightly. Thinking it was one of the train staff, she opened it, only to find Lewis Elliott lounging elegantly outside. The bright, angry glitter had gone from his eyes, and he looked perfectly relaxed. Lorel stared at him suspiciously.

'What do you want?' she said rather ungraciously.

'I thought I'd try another apology,' he said, with that charm that he seemed able to turn on and off at will. His gaze rested on her, with that hypnotic quality which she found so disturbing. Then she straightened her shoulders. She wasn't going to let this man get round her because he had the most gorgeous blue eyes she had ever seen!

On the other hand, though, she had to admit that she hadn't exactly been polite. Perhaps it wouldn't hurt to meet him half-way——'

'There's really no need for you to apologise,' she conceded reluctantly. 'In fact, I was the one who was rude.'

'Yes, you were,' he agreed. 'But perhaps it was my fault for boring you with my family problems.'

'You didn't bore me. But I certainly didn't like the way you were dealing with those problems!'

Lewis merely shrugged. 'You're in no position to make any judgement. You don't know either my stepbrother, or Melinda.'

'I know that you haven't got the right to interfere in someone else's life,' she retorted.

The first flicker of response showed on his face, revealing itself in a faint tightening of his mouth.

'What am I meant to do? Stand aside and watch Felix get deeply involved with someone who's completely unsuitable?'

'She's only unsuitable in *your* opinion,' Lorel reminded him sharply. 'What gives you the right to make that sort of judgement?'

'Perhaps the fact that I've been sorting out the problems in my stepbrother's life since he was a teenager,' Lewis replied drily.

'Maybe you should have let him deal with his own problems. Then he might have been able to run his own life more successfully when he was an adult.'

Lewis raised one eyebrow. 'I very much doubt it. But I didn't come here to discuss Felix's lack of taste in women. I wanted to ask you if you'd join me for dinner this evening.'

His invitation came as a complete surprise. Lorel lifted her head and looked at him with a touch of exasperation. 'I just don't understand you,' she admitted frankly.

'Good,' he said, with some satisfaction. 'We'd be in for a very boring evening if we didn't have anything left to discover about each other.'

Lorel was very much aware of the charm oozing out at full strength now. She tried valiantly to resist it, but was very hard.

'*Why* do you want to take me to dinner?' she demanded.

'Because I want to see what you look like in that dress,' he said, his gaze shifting to the black velvet. 'My guess is that the result's going to be fairly spectacular.'

'You're crazy,' she said, with a shake of her head.

'My family wouldn't agree with that. They think I'm very staid. Even rather boring.'

Her eyes shot wide open. 'Why on earth do they think that?'

'Because I prefer work to play,' answered Lewis. 'And because I—quite literally—don't have much time for women.'

Her eyes were like saucers now. 'You don't like them?' she said incredulously.

His mouth relaxed into a slow smile.

'To the contrary. I like them a great deal. But for the last couple of years, I've been much too busy to spare time for all the niceties required when one takes out a lady.'

'And now you've suddenly found yourself with a few free hours on your hands, so you've decided to make up for lost time?' she retorted crisply. 'Well, not with me, you don't! Find yourself some other willing female to entertain you for the rest of the journey, Mr Elliott. This particular one has got better things to do!'

She tried to close the door on him, but he easily held it open.

'Why do you keep getting so angry, when all I'm doing is simply telling you the truth?' he asked.

To be honest, she didn't know. Perhaps it was an instinctive defence system, she thought to herself uneasily. Something inside of her was warning her to resort to any measures to stop herself from getting involved with this man. He didn't look dangerous, he didn't sound dangerous—but her nerve-ends recognised some sort of threat, and they were responding accordingly.

'I wish—I wish that you'd leave me alone,' she said at last, in a low voice. 'I'm not sure that I like you very much.'

'But *I* like *you*,' he responded softly.

Lorel gave a shaky sigh. She found him a very confusing, contradictory man. Why wouldn't he just go away and let her be?

As if reading her thoughts with uncanny accuracy, Lewis gave a small shake of his head. 'I'm not going until you agree to have dinner with me tonight.'

'Oh, all right,' she muttered irritably. 'If that's the only way I can get rid of you.'

'That's the most unenthusiastic acceptance of an invitation that I've ever heard,' he mocked her. 'Never mind, I still intend to hold you to it. I'll see you later, in the Restaurant Car.'

To her relief, he finally went after that. Lorel rather weakly closed the door, and then wondered why she hadn't said an outright 'No', instead of rather feebly giving in to him. Probably because very few people— male or female—said no to Lewis Elliott, she decided gloomily.

By the time she finally made her way to the Restaurant Car, she was feeling rather more confident. Perhaps it was because, without any vanity, she knew she looked good. Gold shadow glittered on her eyelids to match the gold thread on her dress, her hair was caught up at the sides with tiny gold clips, and the dress itself fitted like a dream.

Lewis was already waiting for her, and his eyes registered their appreciation as she sat down opposite him.

The meal was terrific, six courses in all, and somehow an entire bottle of wine had disappeared by the time the last plates had finally been cleared away. Lorel tried to remember how much of it *she* had actually drunk, but wasn't quite sure, although the slight muzziness of her head told her it must have been more than her fair share! It was because she had felt nervous, she defended herself. She had needed it to steady herself. And it had worked. She felt great now, sort of sparkling and very relaxed.

'Why are you travelling on your own?' Lewis asked her. 'Why not with a girlfriend—or boyfriend?'

'I don't have a boyfriend,' she said cheerfully. 'Not at the moment. And none of my friends had any holiday leave due to them. Not that they could have afforded this trip, anyway,' she added frankly.

'But you could?' he observed. 'You must have a very good job.'

Lorel grinned. 'Not any more. I didn't have any holiday leave due, either. I was determined to come, though, so I just chucked in my job, and packed my bags.'

Lewis looked rather surprised. 'Can you afford to do that?'

'Of course,' she said airily. 'I've just received a legacy—that's how I paid for this holiday.' She leant forward, and gave him a confidential smile. 'I'm an heiress.'

He didn't look very impressed, which was rather annoying. Lorel wondered if she had overdone it a bit. She had certainly embroidered on the truth fairly dramatically. There was just enough left of the small legacy from her great-aunt to pay for her holiday in Venice, and then that would be it. Still, there was no need for Lewis to know that. Tonight, she felt curiously liberated, free to be whoever and whatever she wanted to be. And she fancied being rich, mysterious, sophisticated—all the things that she didn't have a hope in hell of being on an ordinary day. She had a feeling that the wine was partly to blame for the odd mood she was in, but it didn't worry her. In the morning, she would be sober and rather dull again. In the meantime, she was thoroughly enjoying herself.

'Want to come along to the Bar Car for a nightcap?' invited Lewis.

'Why not?' She smiled back at him. She got to her feet as gracefully as she could, which wasn't too easy on a moving train and after rather too much wine. Still, she thought she had made a pretty good job of it, and she caught several men glancing in her direction as she left the Restaurant Car, which was rather gratifying.

When they reached the Bar Car, they found it much more crowded than it had been earlier. And the grand piano at the far end was now in use, being expertly played by a small, dark-haired man.

'Perhaps we should avoid the champagne this time,' suggested Lewis, his eyes briefly gleaming.

'I think that's a good idea,' Lorel agreed hurriedly. 'In fact, I think I'll stick to wine, if you don't mind.'

They found a couple of empty seats in one of the small alcoves, and eased themselves in. There wasn't a lot of room, and Lorel found herself wedged up quite close against Lewis. She couldn't inch away again without making her withdrawal seem very obvious, and anyway, it wasn't altogether unpleasant. She gave a small shrug, had some more wine, and decided that she could easily cope with it for a while longer.

The evening passed pleasantly and easily enough. Then later on, a couple of the staff began to move back some of the armchairs, leaving a clear space in front of the bar.

'What are they doing that for?' asked Lorel curiously.

'They're making enough room to dance.'

'People want to dance on a *train*?' she said disbelievingly.

'Why not? Want to try it?'

'Sure,' she said, after only a moment's hesitation. 'I'm in the mood to try anything tonight!'

She didn't see the odd look Lewis gave her, and by the time she turned to him again his face was clear.

The piano player began to churn out some rather schmaltzy waltzes, and several couples shuffled round roughly in time to the music. There wasn't room for any fancy steps, and Lorel soon discovered that she had to stay very close to Lewis, or she started bumping into people. Oh, well, she thought philosophically, she couldn't come to much harm here, right in the middle of this crowded Bar Car. She wound her arms around Lewis's neck and shifted still nearer, making room for another couple who had just wandered on to the makeshift dance-floor.

She had meant to keep their physical contact well short of anything too intimate, but the swaying of the train made it impossible to control all her movements, and somehow she kept getting much closer than she had intended. Or perhaps it was the wine making her unsteady on her feet, she thought with a suppressed giggle. She really shouldn't have had that last glass!

Lewis was a very nice man to hold on to, though, she decided. Sort of solid and warm. Strong, too, and obviously well-built. Oops, she told herself with another small giggle, better stop thinking along those lines, or she might get carried away! She could see the headlines—'Heiress ravishes top industrialist on Orient Express.' She actually laughed out loud at that, and Lewis shot her a quizzical glance.

'What's the joke?'

'Er—nothing,' she said rather hurriedly. 'Look, I think I've had enough of the dancing, the wine—of everything,' she said a little ruefully. 'It's time I went back to my cabin. Thanks for a great evening. I really enjoyed it.'

'Even though you didn't expect to?' he said gravely.

'Well—no,' she admitted. She looked round. 'I'll just get my bag——'

'I'll fetch it for you.' He returned with it a few moments later. She gave him a smile of thanks, and then began to make her way out of the Bar Car. It wasn't until she had actually gone out of the door that she realised he was still behind her.

'Don't you want to stay for a while longer?' she said, surprised. 'Perhaps have a couple more drinks?'

'I've had all the alcohol I need,' Lewis said softly. 'Come on, I'll see you to your cabin.'

Lorel raised her eyebrows. 'I was wrong about you. You *are* a gentleman.'

'Am I?' he said, with a small quirk of his mouth.

Afterwards, she realised that something in his tone, something in the look on his face, should have warned her. At the time, though, she still felt relaxed and cheerful, and even willing to go along with the goodnight kiss that she suspected he might want before he left her.

They reached her cabin door, and she opened it. 'Goodnight,' she said, with a friendly smile.

'No—not just yet,' Lewis said with unexpected abruptness. He gave her a gentle push inside; then he followed her in and closed the door.

It was funny how very quiet and private it seemed once they were in her cabin. It was hard to believe they were on a train, with a couple of hundred other people.

With one easy movement, Lewis pulled down the brocade blinds. 'Just in case we stop at one of the stations,' he said, with a faint smile. 'I think I can do without an audience.'

Lorel was looking at him a little warily now. Although still flushed with wine, she wasn't so befuddled that she couldn't see this situation could easily get out of hand.

And the cabin seemed smaller than ever with Lewis inside it. She felt as if she couldn't move without touching him.

'Nervous?' he said perceptively. 'But you did say you were in the mood to try anything tonight.'

'Did I really say that? I must have been joking——' she gabbled rather hurriedly.

'Let's find out,' came his quiet reply. One step forward was all it took to bring him uncomfortably close, and Lorel was sure she could already feel the heat radiating out from his body. And his eyes—they had gone so very dark, warning her that he was far less calm and in control than he appeared.

There was no room to back away, though. And he looked as if he was in no mood to let her go anywhere, except into his arms.

Although she had been expecting it, it still came as a shock when he actually made his move. Yet she quickly discovered that it wasn't an unpleasant shock. In fact, it was nice. Very, *very* nice.

His kisses were expert, but not deliberately manipulative. She had the feeling that he hadn't planned this. That, even now, he wasn't quite sure where it would lead them to. She had a good idea, though. Which was why she had to put a stop to it now, while there was still time——

Yet she didn't want the kisses to stop. Nor the touch of his hands, which were stroking the soft black velvet of her dress, but in reality, she knew, feeling the even softer promise of her skin underneath.

'I told you that you were my type,' he murmured rather thickly. 'But I didn't realise quite how much. Lorel, I——'

He didn't bother to finish what he had been going to say. There was no need, because both of them knew exactly what he meant. From out of nowhere had come something that neither of them had really expected. What had started off as fun, a gentle contest, was rapidly turning into something very different. The quality of his kisses changed, becoming deeper and fiercer, and she meant to turn her head away, but instead found herself responding. His hands moved again, exploring curves and hollows, and then delving underneath the black velvet, as if impatient for the touch of silky skin instead of synthetic material.

Lorel's head began to whirl. It's the wine, she told herself giddily. Normally, you'd never be behaving like this with a stranger; would never let him do these things to you...

But Lewis didn't feel, or smell—or taste—like a stranger. In fact, it was frightening just how familiar

he seemed. She forgot that there had been times when
she had disliked him, been nervous of him. Her own
hands began to move in eager exploration, and she
heard the breath catch in his throat as the heat between them spiralled into outright flames.

There was no mistaking the wildly clamouring mes-
sages she was getting from him now. Or the answer
he was getting back from her. She felt drugged,
languid, aching—and the pressure of his mouth, the
touch of his fingers, didn't bring relief, but only stirred
up more unfamiliar responses that shivered their way
through her.

Lewis shrugged off his jacket and undid his tie, but
it was her own fingers that slid open the buttons on
his shirt.

'Keep touching me,' he murmured shakily, and she
did; she just couldn't seem to stop. The black velvet
dress slithered to the floor, and his palm urgently
rubbed against the newly exposed skin, forcing a fresh
groan out of her.

The narrow bed was just behind her, and in seconds
they were lying on it. His hands were constantly on
the move now, provoking pleasure after pleasure, each
touch more sweetly intimate than the last. It wasn't
until his full weight crushed down on her that a little
common sense began to filter back into Lorel's giddily
spinning head. She made a half-hearted attempt to
push him away, but he caught hold of her wrists and
let the full force of his vivid blue eyes blaze down at
her.

'Don't turn away from me,' he muttered. 'Let me.
Let me——'

The moment she looked back into his eyes, she was
lost. His weight increased, became an insistent

pressure that turned into a sudden wave of physical delight, and then another, and another...

The train rattled on through the night, but Lorel wasn't aware of it; she wasn't aware of anything except the storm in this man's body rising to a crescendo and, incredibly, her own rising to match and meet it in a hot, harmonious rapture that shook her to the very depths of her soul.

CHAPTER THREE

WHEN Lorel opened her eyes in the morning, she had the worst headache she could ever remember. On top of that, the bed seemed to be moving around. She gave a small groan, and tried to figure out where she was, and what was going on.

Her gaze took in the small, elegantly appointed cabin, and memories began to filter back. She was on a train. No, not just a train—the Orient-Express.

Then she suddenly went very still as she began to remember everything else. The wine, the dancing—Lewis——

She closed her eyes very tightly. It couldn't have happened. It *couldn't*! She would never have done anything like that.

She forced herself to sit up, and then she looked warily around the small cabin. There was no sign that Lewis had ever been there. None of his clothing—so hastily discarded last night—had been left behind, and the connecting door between their two cabins was tightly closed. Lorel shook her head dazedly. Perhaps it had been a dream. Or a nightmare. Yet her own body told her it had been all too real. It felt languid, content; ached in unfamiliar but not unpleasant ways.

A brief tap on the door made her jump violently. Then she looked around rather wildly. Could she jump out of bed and lock the door before he opened it? She didn't want to see Lewis Elliott right now. In fact, not ever again!

'Breakfast, *mademoiselle*,' called out a polite voice.

She let out a brief sigh of relief. It was only the steward. She pulled the bedclothes up to her chin and, in a rather shaky voice, told him to come in.

He placed the tray beside the bed, and then immediately left again. Lorel looked at the fresh croissants, the jam and marmalade and honey. Then she gave a small shudder. She couldn't face food at the moment. She managed a few mouthfuls of coffee, but even that sat uneasily on her stomach. Rather gingerly, she got out of bed, splashed some cold water on to her flushed face, and then slowly pulled on a dressing-gown.

The brocade blinds that Lewis had drawn last night were still pulled down. She released one, and then flinched slightly as bright sunlight streamed into the cabin. Outside, the sky was a clear azure blue, and she could see pine trees and snow-covered Alps, half-frozen streams, and a cluster of picturesque houses huddled into the valley below. She guessed they were just leaving Switzerland, and normally she would have enjoyed sitting and watching the magnificent scenery through which they were now passing, the early-morning sun making everything glitter with sparkling freshness. This morning, though, she hardly saw it. All she was aware of was that the bright sunlight was hurting her eyes. She drew the blind half-way down again, and then went back to sit in a huddle on the bed.

She didn't even hear the connecting door between the cabins silently open. One moment she was alone, and the next she looked up and found Lewis standing quietly beside her.

Her eyes instantly flashed into life.

'Get out of here!' she snarled at him.

Lewis didn't move an inch. Instead, he stared down at her, his eyes seeming an even more amazing shade of blue this morning, but marred by the frown that now shadowed them.

'I didn't expect that sort of welcome.'

'I'm amazed that you expected any sort of welcome at all!' she threw back at him. 'But if you're still in any doubt at all about the way I feel about you this morning, let's get a couple of things perfectly clear. I don't want you in here, I don't even want to see you. Got that?'

'Yes, I've got it,' he growled. 'But why?'

'Why?' she echoed in astonishment. 'You can't be that thick! I really don't think I need to spell it out for you.'

His first flash of anger had passed, and he seemed dangerously calm now.

'Let's assume that I'm completely unintelligent, and need to have everything explained to me in words of one syllable.'

'All right,' she said angrily. 'I'll put it as plainly as I can. Last night, you waited until I'd had too much to drink, and then you seduced me. I don't like that. And I don't like you! Is that plain and simple enough?'

'Perfectly,' replied Lewis. His voice was taut, but still very controlled. Then the hard line of his mouth relaxed a fraction. 'Seduced,' he repeated thoughtfully. 'That's an old-fashioned word. Are you trying to tell me that you're not a very modern girl, Lorel Parker?'

'That depends on what you call modern,' she retorted. 'Do you mean, do I sleep around? Make a

habit of going to bed with men I've only just met?
No, I don't!'

'I believe you,' he said, much to her surprise. 'Is
that what this is all about? An attack of guilty con-
science, because you behaved out of character? But
any seduction that took place last night wasn't completely one-sided,' he reminded her, making her cheeks
flare brilliant scarlet as she remembered things that
she would much prefer to forget.

'It wouldn't have happened at all if you'd behaved
like a gentleman,' she accused.

'You're the one who decided that I *was* a
gentleman.'

'And I was the one who paid the price for being
wrong!' she retaliated with bitterness.

Lewis searched her face with sudden intentness.
'Was it such a hard price to pay? I got the impression
that you enjoyed it as much as I did.'

'That's hardly the point.'

'Then what is?' There was a trace of impatience in
his voice now, and his mouth had resumed its usual
slightly grim line. She guessed this wasn't the reception he had expected this morning—perhaps he had
even come hoping for a repeat performance of last
night!—but she certainly wasn't going to apologise
for her attitude. He was the one who should be offering any apologies that were due.

'You shouldn't have taken advantage of the fact that
I was drunk,' she said stubbornly.

Lewis looked at her very coolly. 'You weren't drunk.
I wouldn't have touched you if you had been. Yes,
you'd had quite a lot of wine, and you weren't totally
sober. But you knew perfectly well what you were

doing. Whatever excuses you're trying to find for your behaviour last night, don't drag out that one.'

At that moment, Lorel felt that she hated him more than anyone else in the world.

'Then what else made me do—what I did?' she got out through gritted teeth.

Lewis shrugged. 'You want to strip it down to its most basic reason? Then I suppose you'd have to say that we both gave in to a very strong and very common biological urge.'

Lorel stared at him in growing horror.

'I don't have biological urges!' she blurted out.

Lewis gazed back at her for a moment. Then, to her surprise—and annoyance—he suddenly began to laugh.

'Lorel, everyone has them. Every man and woman, since the beginning of time.'

'Not me,' she insisted with some dignity. 'At least, not with someone like—like——'

'Someone like me?' he finished for her. He had stopped laughing now, and a very different expression flickered across his eyes. 'Do you want to explain that a little further?'

No, she didn't want to, not at all. She wished he would just go, before this conversation got even further out of hand. She knew perfectly well that he wasn't going to do that, though. She might not know a lot about Lewis Elliott, but there were some things about him that she was beginning to understand only too well.

'I don't like you,' she muttered at last. 'I've already told you that—several times! You're about the last person on earth I'd choose to—to go to bed with,' she finished, with a burst of defiance.

She didn't like the expression in his eyes at all now, but she couldn't seem to look away from him.

'But we didn't go to bed,' Lewis said evenly. 'We made love. There's a difference—don't you know that?'

'No, I don't know it,' she replied furiously.

He studied her consideringly. 'Then you've certainly got a lot still to learn.'

'Well, don't volunteer to be my teacher,' she retorted. 'That's one job vacancy that's definitely not open!'

'Then where do you suggest we go from here?'

'Nowhere! We'll get off this train, go our separate ways, and try to pretend none of this ever happened.'

'And what if I don't want to do that?' His gaze intensified. 'You're looking at this entirely from your own point of view, Lorel. So far, it's all been what *you* want, how *you* feel about the situation. Aren't you interested in hearing my side of it?'

'Quite frankly, no,' she said bluntly. 'I just want you to get out of here. As far as I'm concerned, last night was a big mistake—and one that I don't intend to make ever again!'

She hoped he couldn't hear the slightly desperate note that had suddenly crept into her voice. In truth, she hardly knew what she was saying, because his physical presence had abruptly begun to affect her with frightening intensity. She couldn't look at his mouth without remembering how his lips had felt against her skin; couldn't listen to his voice without hearing all over again the words he had muttered thickly into her ear. And when he shifted position she went completely tense in case he came nearer. She didn't distrust him. She distrusted herself, and her own

undependable responses where this man was concerned. Her body had never let her down like this
before, and she didn't like it, not one little bit.

Lewis's eyes had already gone very cool, though.
There was no sign of the bright blaze that occasionally lit them, and his features were equally emo-
tionless. She had the feeling that there was a great
deal more he wanted to say, but that he was deliberately holding the words back. She was grateful for
that. She felt that she had had about as much as she
could cope with this morning.

'You seem to have made all the decisions,' he remarked at last, in a very even tone. 'It looks as if I
don't have much choice except to go along with them.'

His words didn't make Lorel feel any more relaxed.
She was sure that he wasn't used to taking such a
passive role, and her muscles went even more rigid as
he shifted position again. He was taking a step towards
the door, though, obviously intending to leave. She
released her breath in a pent-up sigh of relief, and
realised then that she had never really thought he
would leave with so little trouble.

He paused in the doorway, though, and shot one
last cold glance at her.

'Which of us do you think has been the loser in all
of this?' he challenged her tautly. Then he went into
his own cabin, flinging the connecting door noisily
shut behind him.

Lorel stared at the door. Who was the loser? Well,
she was, of course! She had lost her pride and her
self-respect. What could be worse than that?

She locked the connecting door; then she slowly
began to wash and dress. When she had finished, she
sat by the window, watching the scenery of northern

Italy drifting by. She didn't want to leave her cabin and have to speak to other people. And she certainly didn't want to run into Lewis Elliott again.

Just saying his name to herself sent a small shiver running through her nerve-ends. She pressed her palms against her aching head, and wished she had never set foot on this damned train.

A couple of aspirins helped to cure her headache, and her jangling nerves slowly began to settle as the morning slid by. The steward brought her lunch on a tray, and she forced herself to eat a few mouthfuls. She felt a lot calmer now, and almost ready to face the world again. Not that she had a great deal of choice, she reminded herself ruefully. The train would be pulling into Venice very shortly. She couldn't stay hidden away in this cabin for very much longer, even if she wanted to.

She gathered together her luggage, and then cautiously opened the door of her cabin. The corridor outside was empty. She guessed that most people were busily collecting their things together, ready to get off the train.

Her eyebrows drew together resentfully. What a waste of money this trip had been! First, that bad experience on the ferry, when her phobia about water had nearly got the better of her, and then last night's disaster——

Was it such a disaster? murmured a treacherous little voice inside her head.

Yes, it was! she answered herself fiercely. She refused to let herself look at it in any other way.

She sidled past the door to Lewis's cabin, and then noticed that it wasn't quite shut. Was he in there? she wondered tensely. Then her eyes suddenly gleamed.

If not, perhaps she could leave him a small parting gift—something to remember her by. He must have a couple of expensive suits, ready for the business meetings he would be attending in Italy. How unfortunate if a bottle of perfume just happened to spill all over them!

Very carefully, she eased open the door a fraction, intending to draw back instantly if Lewis was still inside. The cabin was empty, though. With a quick glance back along the corridor, she slipped inside, her pulses thumping away much faster than usual.

His suitcase was placed just inside the door. Lorel reached into her handbag for the bottle of perfume she kept there. Then her gaze fixed on the briefcase lined up beside Lewis's suitcase. She knew what had to be in it. The papers he had been working on when he had first boarded the train.

Afterwards, she couldn't have explained what had made her do it. All she was aware of was a strong urge to get back at this man. And what better way than by removing something that was obviously very important to him?

Without thinking, without even making any conscious decision, she picked up the briefcase and backed out of Lewis's cabin. She flung her light mac over it, so no one could see what she was carrying. Then she picked up her own case again, and began to make her way along the corridor.

Since the train was pulling into the station now, other people were beginning to leave their cabins. Lorel moved towards them, deciding it would be best to mingle with them, and get lost in the crowd.

She had almost reached them when a hand reached out from behind and descended on her shoulder.

She didn't have to turn round to find out whose hand it was. She recognised Lewis's touch immediately. Her heart jumped, and then began pounding at top speed. Nervously, she glanced down at the briefcase in her hand. Then she relaxed just a little as she saw it was still completely covered by her mac. Lewis couldn't see it.

'What do you want?' she asked, edginess making her voice sound very sharp.

'Did you really intend to get off this train without saying another word to me?' He sounded a little incredulous, and when Lorel swung round to face him she could see that his features were very dark.

'Of course I did,' she said stiffly. 'I thought I'd made that perfectly clear.'

Lewis shook his head. 'I really misread you, didn't I?' he said slowly. 'That sophisticated act you put on last night was just a front. Underneath it, you were just a child playing at being an adult.'

That remark really got to her. 'I'm not a child!' she denied indignantly. 'You'll soon find that out,' she added, with a gleam of triumph, her fingers closing a little tighter around the handle of the briefcase.

Lewis frowned. 'Exactly what is that meant to mean?'

'Nothing at all,' she said with sudden nervousness, realising that it would be really stupid to make him suspicious. She took a step backwards. She wanted to get away from here, before he discovered his briefcase was missing. He was going to be in a furious temper when he realised it had gone, and she didn't want to be around when that happened. 'Well, see you around,' she said, keeping her voice as casual as she could. 'I'm off now.'

'Not yet, you're not,' he said, a trifle grimly. His fingers closed around her arm, making it impossible for her to move.

'Let go of me,' she hissed. 'Or I'll scream!'

'I don't think so. You don't strike me as the sort of girl who'd make a scene in public.'

Lorel glared at him. He was right, of course. She would just end up half-dead with embarrassment, which would hardly help the situation.

'Well, what do you want?' she snapped.

Lewis regarded her steadily. 'Believe it or not, I do have a sense of responsibility,' he said at last. 'And a rather strong one, at that. Neither of us were very careful last night. I wanted to make sure there wouldn't be any consequences that would make the situation even more difficult than it already is.'

Her face flushed bright red as she realised what he was getting at.

'There's nothing for you to worry about,' she lied.

His gaze caught hers and held it with unexpected force. 'You're sure?'

'Absolutely certain,' she grated back at him. 'Will you let me go now?'

'I suppose I don't have much choice, do I?' His voice sounded oddly regretful. He flicked one last un- fathomable glance in her direction. 'It didn't have to be like this,' he said evenly.

'Oh, yes, it did,' she retorted. 'You made sure of that!' She bent down to pick up her suitcase.

'Let me help you with that.'

'I don't need any help. And particularly not from you!'

His blue eyes briefly blazed with pure anger. 'Then to hell with you,' he said curtly. And, with that, he spun round and strode off along the corridor.

Lorel swallowed hard, and found she was shaking. All that defiance had only been on the surface. Underneath, her nerves were in tatters, and she felt an overwhelming need to get as far away from Lewis Elliott as possible.

She hurried out of the station, almost forgetting that she was still clutching Lewis's briefcase. Then she stood still as she saw that the steps outside the station led down to a wide stretch of water. For a while, she had actually forgotten where she was. Venice—where the only practical way to get around was by boat.

She gave a small groan. That was just about the last thing she needed at the moment—another dose of her least favourite form of transport! She didn't think she would get into a panic this time, though. This wasn't the open sea, only the beginning of the Grand Canal. She would be only yards away from dry land, which should make her feel fairly safe.

Some of the other passengers were heading for the water taxis, but she made for the *vaporetto*, the water bus, which was slower and a lot less comfortable, but definitely much cheaper.

She had booked her hotel in London, and had been given detailed instructions on how to reach it. She dumped her case down beside her in the *vaporetto*, made sure that she knew which stop to get off at, and then lifted her head for her first good look at Venice.

She was aware that this should have been a magical moment, her first sight of what was meant to be the most beautiful city in the world. Unfortunately, a low mist obscured everything except the nearest buildings.

She didn't really care too much, though. She wasn't in the mood for magical moments.

Once she got off the *vaporetto*, it took her ages to find her hotel. She had been warned that Venice was an absolute maze, but she hadn't really appreciated how difficult it would be to find her way around. When she did finally stumble across her hotel, it was purely by accident, and not because she had regained her sense of direction. Then she became even more depressed when she found it was little more than a rooming house.

'I know I told them I wanted somewhere cheap, but this is ridiculous,' she muttered to herself, as she looked up at the dilapidated building set beside one of the smaller canals.

Still, there wasn't much she could do about it. She had been told in London that accommodation in Venice was expensive. Since there hadn't been much money left after she had paid for the trip on the Orient-Express, this was all she had been able to afford. With a small shrug of resignation, she picked up her case and went inside.

The interior was a little more promising; not exactly luxury standard, but very clean. So was her room, even though it was only just big enough to take the single bed, chest of drawers, and small wardrobe that had been crammed into it!

Lorel was beyond caring by now, though. Her mood was getting blacker by the minute, and she shoved her clothes into the drawers, slung Lewis's briefcase into a dark corner of the wardrobe, and then went to stare gloomily out of the window.

If anything, the mist had thickened.

'Another mistake,' she muttered to herself. 'This is obviously the wrong time of the year to come to Venice. OK, so it's not completely crammed with tourists, but that's not much good if you can't even see the damned place!'

Since the hotel provided only accommodation, and not food, she finally had to rouse herself and find somewhere to have a meal. Luckily, there was a small *trattoria* nearby, and for a reasonable sum of money she was given more than she could actually eat. When she finally left to make her way back to the hotel, she felt as if she had pasta coming out of her ears. Then she gave a small groan of dismay as she realised it had begun to rain.

'Oh, this is great!' she grumbled, with a fresh wave of gloom. 'If I'd wanted a week of mist and rain, I could have stayed in England!'

The other rooms in the hotel seemed mostly empty, which didn't surprise her. She guessed that anyone who could afford it would go somewhere more up-market. No one seemed to speak English, and since she didn't know more than half a dozen words of Italian, it took a lot of time and much thumbing through a phrase-book to find out even basic things, such as the location of the bathroom.

Since there wasn't much else to do, she went to bed early and then spent a lot of time staring miserably at the ceiling. This entire holiday had turned out to be a disastrous mistake. A disastrous, *expensive* mistake, she reminded herself with another rush of gloom. She was frittering away the last of her small legacy on these few days in Venice, and when she got back to England she wouldn't even have a job. She must have been mad to have acted so rashly!

And then, on top of everything else, there had been that awful episode with Lewis Elliott. She still couldn't quite believe she had done what she had. Gone to bed with a virtual stranger—and *enjoyed* it. She was too honest to admit that she hadn't. It was only after- wards that she had begun to feel so awful. She had been genuinely shocked by her own behaviour, and by the discovery of a side of herself that she hadn't even known existed.

She tossed and turned for a couple more hours, kept closing her eyes, more in hope than any real belief that she would fall asleep, and then at last drifted into a light doze that slowly deepened into real sleep.

In the morning, she crawled unenthusiastically out of bed, peered out of the window, and then gave a small 'Oh!' of surprise. The rain had stopped, the mist had cleared, and a pale, golden light illuminated the city. The small canal outside her window glittered, the buildings opposite didn't look nearly as dilapi- dated as they had the day before, and she found herself unexpectedly eager to see more of this unashamedly romantic city.

An hour later, she was dressed, had eaten a quick breakfast at a nearby café, and was standing at the side of the canal, poring over the guide-book. She supposed she ought to start with the more obvious sights—St Mark's Square, the Basilica, the Doge's Palace—if only because they would probably be the easiest to find. Rather than try to negotiate her way through the maze of narrow streets, she took the *vaporetto*, and settled back to enjoy the experience of a trip up the Grand Canal.

This morning, Venice seemed a completely dif- ferent city from the one she had arrived in yesterday.

Or perhaps it was her own frame of mind that had changed. Her memories of Lewis Elliott weren't quite so frighteningly vivid as they had been yesterday. In time, she would probably forget him completely, she told herself firmly. And if she didn't really believe that, then she didn't intend to admit that fact.

Instead, she settled back to enjoy the sight of Venice glistening in the early spring sunshine. The *palazzos* slid by, some crumbling, some still impressive, but all of them beautiful. The *vaporetto* passed under the Rialto Bridge, and Lorel looked up to admire it, and then gave a smile of contentment. This was how she had imagined it would be, before Lewis Elliott had stepped in to ruin everything. Well, he wasn't going to spoil the rest of her holiday, she decided with determination. In fact, she wasn't even going to think about him any more.

The Grand Canal wound round, with even more boats filling it now. Sleek black gondolas, small and large motorcraft, water taxis and *vaporetti*, churned their way past. Although the peak of the tourist season was still quite a long way off, it seemed that the city was never less than crowded and busy.

The church of Santa Maria della Salute loomed on the right, looking rather like a giant wedding cake with its ornate white walls, domes and cupolas. They were at the entrance to the Grand Canal now, and on the left was the entrance to St Mark's Square with, just beyond it, the Doge's Palace, a dazzling fantasy in pink and white, with fine stone tracery.

Lorel left the *vaporetto*, along with a couple of dozen other tourists, and headed along with them towards the main square. She had to admit it was very impressive. And very big! The famous cafés which lined it were already open, their chairs and tables set out in the golden and surprisingly warm sunshine. And at the other end was the bright red belltower, and beyond that, the Basilica of St Mark's, with its huge curved portals, its mosaics touched with gold that caught and reflected the sunlight and the five great domes which crowned the famous church.

The square itself was so large that, despite the number of people in it, it didn't seem crowded. Lorel gave a sigh of satisfaction. Although she had seen photographs of the square, it certainly didn't compare to being here in person. She was just trying to decide whether she wanted to tackle the Basilica first, or the Doge's Palace, when a very familiar voice sounded in her ear.

'I thought I'd find you here, if I waited long enough. Everyone who comes to Venice heads first for St Mark's Square.'

Her legs turned to absolute jelly. The one man she hadn't wanted to see ever again. And here he was, right beside her!

Lorel swallowed hard, and tried to get a grip on her shattered nerves. 'Well, fancy seeing you here,' she burbled. 'What a coincidence——'

'Oh, it's no coincidence at all,' Lewis assured her rather grimly. 'I thought I'd already made that very plain.'

Lorel swallowed again. Yes, he had, but she didn't want to think about that.

'This is a fantastic place, isn't it?' she waffled on. 'And the weather's so much better today. I was afraid it was going to rain all week——'

'Where's my briefcase?' he cut in tersely.

'What briefcase?' she asked innocently.

Lewis gave a small growl under his breath. 'I haven't got the time or patience to go through some panto-mime routine. You took it, and both you and I know that. You were seen carrying it when you left the station. The man who saw you had seen us together the night before, and he assumed that you had every right to have it in your possession. He didn't realise that you were stealing it!'

Lorel's eyes flashed. 'I don't steal!' she said sharply. Then she bit her lip. Normally, that was perfectly true. There was something about this man, though, that made her act completely out of character. Could she be blamed for that? she argued with herself fiercely. She managed to convince herself that she couldn't and went back on to the attack again.

'I've had enough of this,' she told him, with some determination. 'I told you on the train that I didn't want to see you again, and I meant it. Go away and leave me alone. I've got a lot of sightseeing planned for today. I don't want to stand around all morning, having silly arguments with you.'

'I intend to stick around until I get back that briefcase,' Lewis informed her grimly. 'I *need* the papers in it. Without them, this trip to Italy will have been a complete waste of time.'

Lorel hoped he couldn't see the gleam of satis-faction that lit up her eyes. Taking that briefcase had been the perfect way to get back at him! All right, she knew she couldn't keep it indefinitely. She had never intended to do that. But she was certainly going to make him sweat for a couple of days, before she finally handed it back to him. Her tongue briefly licked her lips. Revenge certainly was sweet!

'Well, I suppose I can't stop you hanging around, if you've nothing better to do,' she replied airily. 'I just hope you don't get too bored.'

Lewis looked as if he would like to wring her neck, but Lorel knew she was perfectly safe. There were far too many people around for him to risk inflicting any kind of physical injury on her.

Turning away from him, she headed towards the belltower. Leaving Lewis standing at the entrance, she went inside and took the lift up to the top. The view was fantastic, with the sunlit panorama of Venice spread out on all sides. She didn't want to go down again—especially since she was sure Lewis would still be there, waiting for her.

He was, his blue gaze intense and furious. He fell into step beside her as she made her way towards the Basilica, and although she refused to look at him she knew his features were fixed in a black scowl.

'I could go to the police,' he threatened at last.

'Yes, you could,' she agreed. 'But what good would that do? It wouldn't get your briefcase back again.'

'Do you know how important those papers are to me?' he demanded.

Lorel smiled sweetly at him. 'I'm afraid I've absolutely no idea. You know how we females are—no head for business.' She paused under one of the ornate portals leading into the church. 'Are you coming inside, or are you going to stay and simmer in the sun?'

He didn't even bother to answer. Instead, he propped himself up against one of the stone pillars, and Lorel quickly got the message. She could do all the sightseeing she wanted, but she was always going to find him waiting for her when she came out again.

She bit her lip. Was it really worth all this hassle? Then she was immediately angry with herself for even thinking that. Of course it was worth it! She had lost her self-respect, and he had lost his briefcase. It seemed to her an extremely fair exchange. They had both had to give up something of great value.

It was dark inside the church, which suited her mood. The great domes loomed high overhead, their beautiful mosaics almost lost in the shadows. Lorel wandered around without really seeing their sombre splendour. Coming face to face with Lewis again had been far more of a shock than she had been willing to admit, and now that she was no longer bolstered up by that initial burst of defiance she was beginning to feel unpleasantly shaky. She knew she needed to get away from him. She didn't think her nerves would stand it if he trailed around after her all day, like some avenging angel. The only problem was, how was she to manage it?

Her gaze slid round slightly desperately, and then fixed on a large group of tourists at the far end of the church. They were obviously just getting ready to leave, eager to move on to another of Venice's numerous attractions.

Moving quickly, Lorel went over to join them, pushing her way into the very centre of the crowd. As they made their way out of the Basilica, she edged out with them, certain Lewis wouldn't be able to spot her in the middle of the jostling throng.

Once outside, they began to head in the direction of the Doge's Palace. Lorel immediately gave a frustrated groan. She needed to get out of St Mark's Square. While she was here, she would stay trapped.

She glanced round, and saw that Lewis was still staring moodily at the main entrance to the Basilica. She took a deep breath, and hoped he wouldn't turn round and look in her direction at the wrong moment. Then she peeled off from the crowd, scuttled round the side of the Basilica, and shot down a narrow street opposite.

She didn't have the slightest idea where she was going, but she didn't really care. She just kept moving, turning left and then right, dashing across another smaller square and past a church, then off down another narrow road.

There were far less people around now she had left the main tourist area of St Mark's. A couple looked at her curiously as she careered past, but mostly they took no notice.

Out of breath, she paused for a moment and, for the first time, looked back. Then she gave a disbelieving shake of her head. There was a tall, dark, frighteningly familiar figure at the far end of the street—and he was heading purposefully in her direction.

The man was like a limpet! she told herself a little despairingly. It was just impossible to shake him off!

She began to run again and didn't look round any more, but she didn't need to. All her senses were shrieking out that Lewis was only yards behind her.

There was a canal in front of her now, blocking her escape. Then she let out a breathless sigh of relief as she saw a small bridge crossing it. There were steps up one side, and she thundered up them, and then ran across the top of the bridge.

'Lorel—wait!' came Lewis's imperious command.

Not likely! she thought to herself grimly. She galloped down the steps on the far side of the bridge, and had almost reached the bottom when she suddenly missed her footing. The world did a complete somersault, and then she came crashing down so hard that she knocked practically all the breath out of her body. Her head cracked against something solid, a great blackness swooped over her, and with a small groan she let it completely swallow her up.

CHAPTER FOUR

HER eyes fluttered half-open, and then closed again. There was a lot of pain, both inside her head and spreading its way right through her body. She didn't want to move; didn't even want to think. Instinctively, she knew it would hurt far too much.

She seemed to doze for a while, although she thought she probably wasn't completely asleep because she was vaguely aware that she could hear voices. She didn't know what they were saying, but that was because she couldn't be bothered to listen.

Then she gradually realised that someone seemed to be saying a name over and over, which became a little irritating after a while. She decided to ignore it. After all, it wasn't anything to do with her.

Then she did actually fall asleep again. Or it might have been another lapse into unconsciousness. And when she swam back to reality a second time things seemed much clearer. She opened her eyes wide, and slowly looked around.

There was still a thumping pain inside her head, but it didn't seem as bad as it had been before. She blinked a couple of times and waited for everything to slide slowly into focus. Then a small frown wrinkled her forehead. This wasn't her bed—nor was it her room. She wasn't at home, in her own flat. So—where on earth was she?

Another frown creased her face as she tried to figure it out. Not a hospital—everything was too elegant, too grand. Perhaps if she saw more of the room, she would finally recognise it. She tried to move her head, and then gave a small groan as a fresh bolt of pain zipped through it. Very quickly, she closed her eyes again.

'Lorel?' said a voice sharply. 'Are you awake?'

Reluctantly, she forced her aching eyelids open and found herself gazing up at a dark-haired man with piercingly blue eyes. She looked at him groggily. Was he a doctor? But he wasn't wearing a white coat——

'Lorel?' he said again. 'How do you feel?'

He was obviously talking to her, but his words didn't seem to make much sense. Who was Lorel? Was it supposed to be her? With a rising sense of panic, she realised she didn't know. There was an awful blankness inside her aching head, as if it had been completely wiped clean of every thought and every memory.

'Don't know,' she muttered in a shaky voice. She suddenly shivered. 'Don't know!' she repeated, her tone echoing her growing fear.

'Don't know what?' asked the man. His own voice sounded a little impatient now. 'Don't play games, Lorel. I just want to know how you are.'

She licked her dry lips. 'Can't remember,' she muttered, tossing a little restlessly now, even though it hurt to move. 'Not—anything.'

He stared down at her with clear disbelief. 'Are you telling me you've got amnesia?' he queried incredulously.

She couldn't understand why he wasn't helping her. Or fetching someone who would know what to do. She was telling him she was frightened; that the panic was starting to well right through her as the blankness inside her head just seemed to grow and grow; and all he was doing was standing there and looking at her as if he thought she was making the whole thing up.

She tried to tell him how scared she was, how awful it felt to have this terrifying emptiness inside her head, but she couldn't get any words out. Instead, she just gazed up at him in utter misery, feeling ill and alone, and confused to the point where she thought she was going a little mad.

He was still frowning, but his dark features didn't seem quite so forbidding.

'All right,' he said. 'You'd better just lie still and rest. The doctor's coming again later today. Let's hope he can sort out this mess.'

She didn't want to rest. She wanted to get her memory back—and right now! She wanted to know who she was, what she was doing here—and who this unsympathetic man was.

Tiredness was beginning to sweep over her again, though. Not a natural tiredness, but an overwhelming exhaustion of both mind and body. Her eyelids were too heavy to stay open for very much longer but, at the same time, she didn't want to sleep. She was too scared. What if nothing had changed by the time she woke up again? She didn't think she could cope with this yawning emptiness inside her head. It really would drive her insane...

'Go to sleep,' said the man beside the bed. 'I'll stay here with you.'

'All the time?' she mumbled anxiously. 'You won't go away?'

'I won't go away,' he promised. A warm, firm hand closed over her own, and for some reason she immediately began to feel more safe. She still didn't want to go to sleep, but she couldn't resist it any longer. Her eyes slid shut, and she drifted into another long period of dreamless unconsciousness.

When she eventually opened her eyes again, the first thing she was aware of was that someone was holding her hand. A little puzzled, she looked up, wondering who it was. A man with dark hair and vivid blue eyes—he was sitting beside the bed, and looking straight back at her.

'You've been asleep for nearly ten hours,' he told her. 'Do you feel any better than when you last woke up?'

She looked at him blankly. 'I don't remember waking up.'

He gave a brief frown. 'Then you still can't remember anything?'

She wasn't fully awake yet, and couldn't figure out what he meant.

'About what?' she asked, wrinkling her forehead.

His blue gaze seemed to focus on her with fresh intensity. 'Do you know your own name?'

'Of course,' she said, a little annoyed. What did this man think she was? An idiot? 'My name's——' She paused, and for a moment felt a flash of panic as she hunted around in her head for the answer to such a simple question. Then she gave a sigh of relief. 'It's Lorel Parker,' she said with complete certainty.

She was surprised when the man beside the bed looked almost as relieved as she was that she had come up with the right answer.

'Where do you live?' he asked, after a short pause.

Again, she needed time to think about it. Then the address slid smoothly into her memory, and she repeated it to him.

'Why are you asking all these silly questions?' she asked, puzzled.

'Because last time you woke up, you couldn't remember a single thing,' he informed her. 'Not even your name.'

She gave a light grimace. 'I told you, I can't even remember waking up before.' Then she glanced round the room. 'I suppose this is the classic question in this sort of situation,' she said wryly. 'But I've got to ask it, anyway. Where am I?'

'We'll get to that in a minute. Let's get a couple of basic facts established first. Firstly, how do you feel?'

'I've got a headache,' she said slowly. 'And I think I must have some hefty bruises.' She shifted a little uncomfortably. 'I can definitely feel some sore spots. And I'm a bit dizzy. Apart from that, I don't feel too bad. I do want to know how I *got* in this state, though.'

'You still can't remember that?'

'No. There seem to be quite a few blank spots inside my head,' she admitted.

He frowned. 'And I'm one of those blank spots?'

'I'm afraid so.' She looked at him more closely, trying to find something familiar about the clearly defined lines of his face, the rather tense set of his mouth, and the highly distinctive colour of his eyes. For a fraction of a second, something about their intense blue seemed to strike a responsive chord in her; then the sensation faded, and the man appeared a complete stranger again.

'Who are you?' she asked curiously.

'My name's Lewis Elliott.'

It didn't mean a thing to her. 'Are you sure that I know you?' she questioned doubtfully.

'Oh, yes,' came his unexpectedly grim reply. 'You know me.'

Lorel gave a small sigh. 'Well, I suppose it'll all come back to me in time. Until it does, perhaps you'd better fill me in on one or two things. Like where I am,' she added, looking round at the unfamiliar surroundings. 'What is this place? Some kind of private nursing home?' She began to look a trifle worried. 'I really can't afford to stay in a place like this.'

'This is the Palazzo Gregolino,' Lewis told her. 'And since I'm renting it at the moment, there's no question of you having to pay for your stay here.'

But Lorel was already beginning to get totally confused again. 'Palazzo?' she echoed, with a baffled look. 'What do you mean? How can this be a palazzo?'

Lewis's eyes narrowed. 'Where do you think you are? Which city?'

'Well—London, of course,' she replied. 'I've had some kind of accident, haven't I? Been knocked down by a car, or something?'

'No,' he answered, with a touch of curtness. 'You weren't knocked down by a car. Nor are you in London. This is Venice.'

'Venice?' Lorel gazed at him in total bewilderment. 'I don't understand——'

'What's the last thing you remember?'

It was hard to work that out. Big chunks of her memory had come back again, but it all seemed to be floating around inside her head in a rather disordered sequence.

'Going to work, I suppose,' she said rather uncertainly, at last. 'I think that was yesterday.'

'Yesterday, you were lying in this bed for most of the day,' came Lewis's slightly rough response. 'You—you tripped over in the morning, and knocked yourself out. You were out cold for quite a while, but then you came round for a short time in the evening. You couldn't remember anything, though, and eventually you went to sleep. You woke up again about half an hour ago.'

She blinked. It was so hard to take all of this in.

'The doctor's been in to see you a couple of times,' Lewis continued. 'You've got mild concussion, and several large bruises from your fall, but he's satisfied there isn't any serious damage. You're to stay in bed for at least another couple of days, and then take it very easy for a while, until you've completely recovered from the concussion.'

Lorel was still trying to come to grips with what he had told her.

'I'm really in Venice?' she said uncertainly. 'I know I was planning a holiday, but it was all in the future.'

'This *is* the future,' Lewis said, in a quieter voice. 'It's just your memory that's lagging a few weeks behind. The doctor says it's fairly common after a crack on the head. It should all come back to you fairly soon. You've just got to be patient.'

'I suppose it's already starting to get better, if I couldn't remember anything at all last night,' she said, trying to look on the optimistic side of this bizarre situation.

'By tomorrow, there's a good chance you'll be able to recall everything,' Lewis agreed.

She began to ask another question, but Lewis held up one hand.

'I think that's enough for now,' he said decisively. 'The doctor was pretty specific. Plenty of rest for a couple of days, and no stress or strain.'

'It's pretty stressful, having chunks of your life missing,' she complained.

'We'll sort the rest of it out after you've had some sleep. Are you hungry? Or thirsty?'

She was thirsty, but couldn't face food yet. She managed to sip some fresh fruit juice, and then slumped back on the pillows again. Lewis Elliott was right, she realised. She *had* had enough for the moment. She wondered if he was the sort of man who was always right about everything, and decided it would be very irritating if that turned out to be the case. Then she closed her eyes, and promptly went back to sleep.

She didn't sleep for so long this time, and when she woke up again she could clearly remember all of her conversation with Lewis Elliott—whoever he might be! She realised he had told her absolutely nothing about himself, or how he had come to be on the scene.

Very carefully, she sat up, and was pleased to find she felt much better. Her head still ached a bit, and her exploring fingers found the tender, swollen lump where she had obviously hit it when she had fallen. The dizziness had practically gone, though, and she could think fairly straight. With a grunt of satisfaction, she looked around and began to take more notice of the room she was in.

It certainly was elegant! It also shrieked of luxury and comfort. The silken sheets were soft and smooth against her skin; the walls and ceiling were ornately decorated, there were heavy brocade curtains at the windows, and the exquisitely patterned carpet must have cost a small fortune.

She remembered Lewis Elliott telling her that he had rented the *palazzo* for a while. She had a good idea what it must cost to rent a place like this for even a few days, and her eyebrows lifted thoughtfully. Obviously, he was a man with money. What else was there to find out about him?

Almost as if he had heard her unspoken question, the door opened and Lewis Elliott came in. He seemed rather surprised to find her sitting up in bed, but was obviously satisfied with her progress.

'It looks as if you're going to have a fairly quick convalescence,' he remarked. 'How's the memory this morning?'

'Not too bad. Most of the bits seem to be falling into place,' she told him.

That piece of news seemed to please him.

'Good,' he said briskly. 'Then you can tell me what you've done with my briefcase.'

Lorel looked at him blankly.

'Your briefcase?' she repeated. 'Why should I know anything about your briefcase?' Then her face suddenly cleared as one obvious explanation occurred to her. 'Am I your secretary? Is that why I've come with you on this trip to Venice?'

'Damn it, you are *not* my secretary!' Lewis said irritably. 'And you didn't come with me. We met on the train.' He looked angry and frustrated. 'I thought you said your memory was now all right again! It still seems pretty poor to me.' His eyes suddenly flared. 'Or are you just faking the whole thing?' he demanded suspiciously. 'Do you think you can get yourself out of trouble this way, by pretending you can't remember what happened?'

She frowned at him uneasily. 'Trouble? What trouble?'

She saw him make an effort to get his temper back under control. He paced over to the window, and when he turned to face her again she was relieved to see the tension had left his features.

'If you really can't remember anything about the briefcase, then there's not much point in going into it right now.' He shot a curious glance at her. 'Why did you think you might be my secretary?'

'I can remember handing in my notice at my old job,' she explained. 'I thought for a moment that I might have got another job, with you. But that's not right, is it?' she said, her forehead wrinkling as she slowly worked it out for herself. 'I was coming to Venice on holiday—I remember that now.' Her eyes brightened. 'On the Orient-Express. Yes, that was it! Some money I inherited from my great-aunt, and I decided to blow it on the trip of a lifetime. Only now I can't remember any of it,' she finished rather dolefully. 'Did I enjoy the trip?'

'It was—fairly eventful,' Lewis remarked drily. Before she had a chance to ask him exactly what he meant by that, he went on, 'The entire journey's a complete blank?'

'I'm afraid so. I can remember booking the trip, and getting excited about it. I can even remember packing. But that's it. After that—nothing.' Her brows drew together. 'Why do you suppose that is? Everything else is pretty clear in my mind by now. Why not those last couple of days?'

Lewis seemed to hesitate before he answered. 'I don't know,' he said at last, in a distinctly curt tone.

Lorel shrugged. 'Well, I suppose I'm going to have to rely on you to tell me everything that happened. You said we met on the train? Then we must have talked, spent some time together—you'll be able to fill in some of the details for me.'

She had the impression that Lewis's eyes had darkened, although she couldn't figure out why. It seemed a perfectly reasonable thing to ask him, and she didn't think it would be too difficult for him to give her the information she wanted. Perhaps he simply didn't want to be bothered, she told herself with a grimace. Maybe he had decided she had caused him more than enough trouble already, falling over and knocking herself out right in front of him, so that he didn't have any choice except to bring her here and take care of her.

At least, that's what she *assumed* had happened. She didn't really know. Until she managed to remember the missing couple of days for herself, she was going to have to accept Lewis's version of events.

Only, he didn't seem very keen to discuss them. He was silent for a long while after she had asked him to fill in the details. Then he moved a little restlessly over to the window, and finally spoke to her from there.

'We met on the train, then got to know each other rather better on the ferry crossing. You were—nervous of the sea,' he said briefly. 'You said your parents had drowned, and that had given you a phobia about water.'

'I told you about my parents?' she said, startled.

'No details, only the basic facts. When we rejoined the train at Boulogne, we had a couple of drinks, and

later had dinner together.' Again, there was an odd
hesitation which made her feel distinctly uneasy. 'That
was about it,' he finished rather abruptly. 'We parted
when the train reached Venice, and didn't make any
more plans to meet.'

'Then how come you were around when I fell?' she
asked curiously.

Lewis shifted position, as if he found it difficult to
stand still. In fact, she had the impression that he
would prefer to be almost anywhere at this moment,
except in this room with her.

'We met in St Mark's Square.' He gave a non-
committal shrug. 'Everyone who comes to Venice
makes their way to St Mark's Square. It wasn't so
odd that we should meet there.'

'Was that where I had my accident?'

'No, it was a short distance from there. You tripped
crossing one of the small bridges. I was—I just happened to be behind you, and saw it happen.'

'And came rushing to my rescue? I really am very
grateful,' she told him.

Lewis gave a small grunt, and turned away.

'Why didn't you take me to my hotel?' she went
on. 'Surely it would have been less trouble for you?'

'I didn't know where you were staying. Anyway——' He stopped rather suddenly, as if he didn't
want to say any more.

She decided it was no good pushing him. He obviously wouldn't tell her any more than he wanted her
to know. All the same, it was rather peculiar. She was
quite sure he wasn't telling her the entire truth. But
why not?

She gave a brief frown.

'What was all that earlier about a briefcase? Have
you lost one?'

'You could say that,' he replied grimly.

'But what's it got to do with me?'

There was another of those brief pauses which she
was beginning to find distinctly worrying. She was
certain that Lewis Elliott was keeping quite a lot back
from her. What, though? And *why*?

'I thought that you might be able to help me find
it,' he replied at last. 'But until you get your memory
back completely, there isn't much chance of that.'

Lorel slowly shook her head. She still didn't really
understand any of this. Then she gave a small shrug.
There wasn't much point in bothering her head about
it right now. When she remembered the missing couple
of days, she would know what this was all about.

In the meantime, what she would really like was to
freshen up.

'Is there a bathroom around here?' she asked.

'Just through there,' replied Lewis, nodding towards
a door on the far side of the room. 'Need any help?'

'No, thanks,' Lorel assured him hurriedly.

Moving slowly and carefully, she pushed back the
bedclothes and swung her legs over the side of the
bed. Then she looked down at herself. 'What on earth
am I wearing?' she asked blankly.

An unexpected smile touched Lewis's mouth. 'It was
difficult to find anything suitable at such short notice.
That nightdress belongs to Maria—she's the house-
keeper. She's also a fairly big woman,' he finished
tactfully.

That was obviously something of an under-
statement! The nightdress was huge and, as Lorel gingerly levered herself into an upright position, she had

to hang on to it to stop it slipping down and revealing far more than she was prepared to let Lewis Elliott see.

Then another thought struck her. 'Who undressed me?' she demanded suspiciously.

Lewis's blue eyes glittered. 'Maria, of course,' he answered smoothly.

Lorel wasn't at all sure that she believed him. This was hardly the time to argue about it, though. Instead, with as much dignity as she could manage under the circumstances, she clung on to the voluminous nightdress and made her way across the bedroom, then through the doorway that led to the bathroom.

Once inside, her eyebrows shot up. '*Very* impressive,' she murmured under her breath. And so it was. An absolutely massive bath, gold taps and fittings, and beautifully patterned tiles on the floor and walls.

'All right?' queried Lewis.

Lorel jumped. She hadn't realised he had followed her, and was now standing just outside the door.

'Fine,' she said quickly. Then she firmly closed the door, shutting him out.

She walked over to the sink, and turned on one of the gold taps. Then she splashed the cold water over her face, which for some reason was suddenly feeling rather flushed.

When she lifted her head again and looked in the mirror, she was relieved to find that she didn't look very different from usual. The bump on her head was just on the hairline, and was more or less covered by the soft fall of her hair. Peering under the nightdress, she could see dark bruises on her skin, but they would fade in a few days. All in all, she had been pretty lucky, coming out of that bad fall with very few injuries.

Except that she still couldn't remember those missing couple of days, she reminded herself with a frown. That was definitely rather worrying. All right, Lewis Elliott had filled her in on the basic details. She couldn't quite get rid of the conviction, though, that he hadn't told her the complete truth. The furrow between her brows deepened. Why would he keep anything back from her? She didn't know, and it bothered her. In fact, she was willing to admit that Lewis Elliott himself bothered her. She knew she ought to be grateful to him for bringing her here and making sure she had medical treatment. There was something about him, though—something about those vivid eyes of his...

She shook her head in frustration. She supposed it would all come back to her, in time. She just had to be patient, and wait.

When she finally made her way back to the bedroom, she was rather relieved to find that Lewis Elliott was no longer there. She climbed into bed, and was just settling herself comfortably back on to the pillows when the door opened and a massive woman waddled in.

It wasn't hard to guess that this was Maria, who had donated the nightdress. She was carrying a tray, which she set down beside the bed as she launched into an absolute flood of Italian.

'I'm sorry,' Lorel said rather bemusedly. 'I don't understand a single word. Er—*non capisco.*'

Maria beamed, gestured towards the tray, and launched into another flood of words.

'Well, I guess I get the gist,' Lorel grinned back at her, and she picked up the tray. As she began to eat, Maria nodded in satisfaction, and then waddled out again.

For the next couple of days, Lorel didn't do much except eat, rest and sleep. She was extremely bored by the end of it, but was determined to behave sensibly. More than anything, she wanted to get completely better—and get out of here. For some reason, she felt deeply uneasy about staying at the Palazzo Gregolino and having to sleep under the same roof as Lewis Elliott.

It was because he was a complete stranger, she told herself defensively. Anyone would feel awkward at having to share a house with someone they had never met before. Then she would have to remind herself that she *had* met Lewis Elliott. That, according to him, they had spent quite a lot of time together on the train journey to Italy.

At that point, though, Lorel always ran up against a familiar brick wall. No matter how hard she tried—and it was very hard indeed!—she couldn't remember a single second of that journey. The rest of her memory was working perfectly by now. She could recall absolutely everything, right up to the morning of her departure for Italy. She could remember packing her clothes, and getting a taxi to the station. She had a crystal-clear memory of walking on to the platform, checking in and handing over her luggage. But after that—nothing! The next thing she could remember was waking up in this luxurious bed here, at the *palazzo*.

The doctor had been back to check on her again, and was apparently very pleased with her progress.

At least, that was what Lewis had told her. Since she spoke no more than a dozen words of Italian she had picked up from the phrase-book, and the doctor spoke no English, they had both had to rely on Lewis to translate for them.

After the doctor had prodded and poked her, asked a lot of questions, and then pronounced himself very satisfied with her progress, Lorel turned to Lewis rather impatiently.

'What's he got to say about the fact that I still can't remember a thing about those last couple of days?'

Lewis hesitated for a moment, and then spoke to the doctor in what seemed to be fluent Italian. The doctor shrugged, made a small gesture with his hands, and then launched into a lengthy answer.

'What did he say?' demanded Lorel, when the flood of words finally stopped.

'That it's fairly common for a knock on the head to be accompanied by a temporary loss of memory,' Lewis replied.

The doctor added something else. When Lewis didn't immediately translate, Lorel stared at him.

'Well?' she questioned. 'What else did he say?'

A brief frown touched Lewis's already rather grim face. 'He says that you might not want to remember,' he said shortly. 'That if something—unpleasant happened during those couple of days, then you might prefer to push it right out of your mind, so you don't have to think about it.'

'What do you mean—unpleasant?'

Lewis gave a rather irritable shrug. 'I've no idea. I'm merely translating what the doctor said.'

He seemed in a very odd mood today. Lorel wondered if he was perhaps tired of having her hanging
around, causing him a lot of extra bother and worry.

The doctor smiled at her, added something else in
a soothing voice, and then left the room.

'He says you're to stay in bed one more day,' translated Lewis. 'Then you can get up, as long as you
don't rush around doing anything too strenuous.'

Lorel pulled a face. 'I'm fed up with sitting around,
waiting for things to put themselves right. I don't *like*
losing a couple of days out of my life. As well as that,
it's very inconvenient. I don't even know which hotel
I checked into after I arrived in Venice, so I can't even
get hold of my clothes.' She pulled at the baggy nightdress in disgust. 'How can I get up when I haven't
got anything to wear? Or is Maria going to volunteer
to lend me a dress?'

Lewis's mouth relaxed into a faint smile. 'I think
we'd better try and find you something that'll fit a
little better.'

'I want my *own* clothes,' she insisted. 'And I want
to get out of here, go back to my hotel, and get on
with my holiday. I'm sorry if that doesn't sound very
grateful, considering all the trouble I've put you to,
but that's the way I want things to be.'

She looked at Lewis, to see how he was taking her
bald announcement, and found that his face had
changed yet again. This time, she didn't particularly
like the expression that had settled across his features.
It was unpleasantly dark, and his eyes were fixed on
her rather too intently for comfort.

'How about if we talk about what *I* want for a
change?' he said, his tone as altered as his face.
'You're well enough to face a few facts by now; I don't

have to treat you like an invalid any longer. So—how about if we discuss my briefcase, Lorel?'

Her brows drew together. What did his briefcase have to do with all of this?

'You went on about that once before,' she said rather crossly. 'And I told you that I didn't have the slightest idea what you were talking about.'

Lewis's eyes narrowed. 'That's what you said,' he agreed. 'But what if you're faking this amnesia? It would certainly be one way of getting yourself out of a whole lot of trouble.'

She glared at him in indignation. 'You think I faked that fall?'

'No, not the fall,' he conceded. 'But the loss of memory certainly came at a very convenient time for you.'

Lorel shook her head. 'That's the most incredible thing anyone's ever said to me!' Then she glared at him. 'Do you know what it's like to have a chunk of your life missing? To keep wondering what went on— what you did—during those missing couple of days?' Her eyes narrowed. 'But you *know* what I did, don't you?' she said, more slowly. 'That's what this is all about. You've told me some of it, but there's a whole lot more that you've left out. I'm right, aren't I? You're keeping something back. Well, perhaps you'd better start to fill in some of those gaps!'

Lewis came closer, so that he was looming over her. She flinched a little at the stormy lines of his face, but didn't back away from him. His blue gaze locked on to hers, and the full force of his glittering eyes bore down on her.

'You want to know what you did during those missing couple of days?' he said in a clipped, angry

voice. 'You stole my briefcase! You're a thief, Lorel!'
Ignoring the shocked look that swept over her face,
he went on, 'I *need* the papers and contracts in that
case. I don't know if you're faking this loss of memory
or not and, to be truthful, I don't really give a damn
one way or the other. But I will tell you this. Until I
get back that briefcase—and the papers inside it—I
don't intend to let you out of my sight. One way or
another, I'm going to force you to remember where
you put that case. And believe me, I don't care how
I have to go about it!'

With that, he wheeled round and strode out of the
room, leaving Lorel to stare after him in shaken
disbelief.

CHAPTER FIVE

FOR a few minutes after Lewis had gone, Lorel was sorely tempted to leave the *palazzo* and just make a run for it. Anything to get away from Lewis Elliott and his insane accusations. Then common sense slowly prevailed. Wearing nothing except Maria's nightdress? She wouldn't get very far! The Italian police would almost certainly stop and question a girl hurtling through the streets of Venice wearing just a nightie that was a dozen sizes too big for her!

At the thought of the police, she suddenly shivered. She knew that Lewis Elliott had lied, she wasn't—couldn't be—a thief. Yet the thought of getting caught up in the police system of a foreign country, where she didn't even speak the language, was a distinctly daunting one. There could be all sorts of misunderstandings, and she could inadvertently end up in real trouble. She glanced around the luxurious room, and then shivered again. Anyway, who knew what sort of influence Lewis Elliott might be able to exert? He was obviously a very wealthy man, and he probably had a lot of powerful connections. Who was going to accept her word against his?

She spent the rest of the day trying to figure a way out of this mess, but couldn't seem to come up with any solution. Until she could remember what had happened during those missing couple of days, she was at a very real disadvantage.

Half-way through the next morning, there was a brief knock on her door. Then it opened, and Lewis came into the room.

Lorel was sitting in a chair by the window. The Palazzo Gregolino was situated on one of the smaller side canals, yet there was still plenty to see. Different boats were passing by all day long, and Lorel spent a lot of time just watching the groups of tourists, and the busy Venetians going about their everyday affairs. The sight of Lewis quickly distracted her from the scene outside the window, though.

'What do you want?' she asked, not caring in the least that she sounded very rude.

He tossed a couple of bags on to the bed. 'I've brought you some clothes.'

Instantly, Lorel brightened up. 'You've managed to find out where I'm staying? You've been round to collect some of my things?'

'No, I haven't,' Lewis growled. 'I've phoned round dozens of hotels, but none of them have got a Lorel Parker registered there.' He gave a frustrated gesture with his hands. 'It's like trying to find a needle in a haystack. Practically every other house in Venice takes in paying guests. If you're staying in one of the cheaper rooming houses, then I could be on the phone for a week, and still not come up with the right one.'

'Well—thanks for trying,' she said a little grudgingly.

Lewis shrugged. 'I'm not doing it for any philanthropic reasons. I'm hoping that if I can locate your hotel, I'll find my briefcase. My guess is that you've got it stashed away in your room.'

'That damned briefcase again!' she muttered in annoyance. 'Is it *that* important?'

'Yes, it is,' he replied sharply. 'I'm in Italy on a mixture of business and pleasure, combining a few days' holiday with some very important business meetings. Without the papers in that briefcase, I'm going to be at a distinct disadvantage at those meetings, and I can't afford that.'

'Well, I'm sorry about that, but I don't see how I can help.'

His gaze slid over her assessingly. 'Don't you?'

She glared back at him hotly. 'And what's that meant to mean?'

'Just that I'm still not sure if your amnesia's genuine or not.'

'Oh, it's real enough!' she flung back at him. 'Although perhaps it's a good thing. I'm not sure that I want to remember *you*!'

The blue of Lewis's eyes seemed to deepen several shades. 'But that's exactly what you're going to do,' he informed her softly. Then he gestured towards the clothes on the bed. 'You might as well get dressed. If you're well enough to argue with me, then you're well enough to get up.'

He swung round and left before she had a chance to answer. Lorel wished she could throw something after him, to help work off her temper. Regretfully, she decided that might not be a very good idea. Instead, she sat back in her chair and indulged in a fierce fit of sulking.

Eventually, though, her gaze began to drift over to the bags that Lewis had dumped on the bed. She wasn't interested in whatever was inside them, she told herself with some determination, and forced herself to ignore them for a while longer. Then curiosity finally got the better of her, and she went over to take a closer look.

As she up-ended the bags on to the bed, the clothes inside fell out in a cascade of bright colour. Lorel's eyebrows shot up. This wasn't chainstore stuff! She picked up a thin silk top, and then found the matching skirt. There weren't any price tags attached, but she had a good idea what clothes like this must cost. Each item was beautifully made, the design kept deliberately simple so that it could be worn anywhere, and for any occasion.

A smaller bag revealed lace-trimmed undies, and a nightdress of pure silk. Lorel wondered who had chosen the clothes. Probably not Maria, she thought with a wry smile. The big, cheerful Italian woman always wore shapeless cotton dresses in riotously vivid colours. Had Lewis picked them out himself? Lorel held up the nightie again, and raised her eyebrows at the rather disgraceful concoction of lace and silk. She certainly hoped not! A man would only choose something like this if he was looking forward to seeing it worn.

He most likely had a ladyfriend who had gone round and picked out a few suitable items, she comforted herself. A man like Lewis Elliott would never be short of female companions. He probably had them dotted all round Venice! All he had to do was ring one up and ask her to do him a favour.

The next question was—did she intend to wear these clothes? She gave a grimace. Did she have any choice? The answer to that was pretty obvious—no. If she wanted to leave this room, then she had to put on one of these outfits.

She bathed in the huge tub, dried herself on the soft towels that had been provided, and then wriggled into the underwear, which fitted perfectly. She guessed Lewis had taken the sizes from the clothes she had been wearing when she had first been brought to the *palazzo*, after her fall.

She chose the outfit which looked the least expensive, a plain dress in a shade of green which she knew would perfectly complement her gold-brown hair and eyes. There was a knitted jacket which matched it, and she decided to slip that round her shoulders in case the spring sunshine outside suddenly disappeared, and the weather grew cool. The dress looked sensational. It was a shame she wouldn't be able to keep it. It was the kind of thing she would have loved to have had in her wardrobe, if she could have afforded it.

When she was finally ready, she opened the bedroom door and made her way down the curved staircase which led down to the ground floor. Then she found herself confronted by half a dozen ornately carved doors.

One stood half-open, so she headed towards it. Pushing it wide open, she found a large dining-room with a long, beautifully polished table laid ready for lunch. After a moment's hesitation, she went inside and sat down.

A couple of minutes later, footsteps sounded outside. Then Lewis walked into the room.

When he saw her sitting there, he briefly paused. His gaze slid over her, from her gleaming curls, down over the curves of her body, to the slim line of her ankles. Lorel waited tensely for him to make some very personal remark. Instead, though, his eyes flicked back to her face, his gaze very cool and rather distant.

'I see you made it down to lunch, then,' he observed.

'Of course I did,' she replied stiffly. 'I feel fine now. I want my life to get back to normal as soon as possible.'

Lewis seated himself opposite her. 'Then what are your plans?'

His question rather threw her, because she didn't actually have any yet.

'I don't know,' came her reluctant admission. 'It's all a bit difficult, since I don't have the slightest idea which hotel I booked into after I arrived in Venice. I don't even have any clothes, except these that you've lent me. Incidentally,' she went on, 'where did you get them from?'

'A small boutique just around the corner,' replied Lewis. 'I phoned them up, gave them your age, size and colourings, and asked them to send round a selection of suitable things.'

'I wish they'd sent something cheaper,' she told him bluntly.

Lewis shrugged. 'I didn't set any price limit. Anyway, it isn't important.'

'It is to me,' she insisted. 'These clothes are *expensive*. I don't feel right wearing them.'

'Why not? They look good on you, and surely that's all that matters.'

'But I haven't paid for them myself! I *can't* pay for them.'

His eyes briefly gleamed. 'On the train, you told me that you were an heiress. Are you now saying that you weren't strictly truthful with me, Lorel?'

'I've no idea what I told you on that train,' she reminded him with some exasperation. 'Except I'm sure I never said anything so stupid. Why would I have told such a silly lie?'

'Perhaps you wanted to impress me,' Lewis suggested.

'That's ridiculous!' she retorted. 'I wouldn't want to impress you!'

'No?' he queried, a faint smile hovering around the corners of his mouth. 'But you can't really remember, can you?' came his gentle gibe. 'You don't even know if it worked. For all you know, I might have been very impressed indeed.'

Lorel sniffed. 'Because you thought I was rolling in money?'

His gaze rested on her in a way that she found quite unnerving. 'Not necessarily,' he replied in a silky voice.

She decided that she didn't like the drift of this conversation. Luckily, Maria came in a moment later, carrying a tray loaded with plates of salad and bowls of fruit.

She beamed at Lorel, and chattered away to her as she set out the plates.

'Maria's pleased to see you up and about, and looking so well,' translated Lewis.

'Thank you—*grazie*,' Lorel smiled back at her.

Maria turned back to Lewis, and spoke to him at length in a much sterner tone. Then she picked up the empty tray, and left the room.

'What was that all about?' asked Lorel curiously.

Lewis shot her a dry glance. 'The general gist of it was that I'm to behave like a perfect gentleman. Maria doesn't approve of the two of us being under the same roof. In fact, I don't think she even approves of the two of us eating together like this. In her opinion, you should be very strictly chaperoned while you're staying at the *palazzo*.'

'And do you think I need to be chaperoned?' enquired Lorel, looking back at him coolly.

'That rather depends.'

'On what?'

'On how you behave yourself while you're here,' he replied calmly.

Lorel instantly bristled, because his insinuation had been clear enough. 'What do you think I'm going to do?' she demanded. 'Throw myself at you? Do you really think that *I'm* the one who's going to make the advances?'

'I've no idea. I don't know you well enough yet, Lorel Parker.'

'Oh, I've had enough of this,' she muttered. She tossed down her napkin, and got to her feet. 'I don't want to eat with you, and I've had just about enough of your so-called hospitality. I'm getting out of here—and right now!'

She started to leave the room, but as she walked past Lewis he reached out and caught hold of her wrist.

'You're not going anywhere,' he informed her steadily.

Lorel flung an angry glance at him. 'Just try and stop me!'

'I'm doing that already,' he pointed out. And so he was. She wriggled furiously, but there was no way she could break the strong grip of his fingers.

'So, what are you going to do?' she demanded defiantly. 'Hold me like this indefinitely?'

'No. Just until we've got a few things straight.'

She tried wrenching her hand away again, but then gave up. He was right. She was going nowhere until he let go of her. She flopped sulkily down into the chair beside him. Instantly, he let go of her wrist.

'That's better,' he said approvingly. 'Now, do you want to eat first, or shall we discuss the arrangement I've got in mind for you?'

'I think I'll eat,' she replied, glaring at him with pure dislike. 'I don't know what you're going to tell me, but I bet it'll ruin my appetite!'

The salad was fresh and delicious, and the wine that accompanied it was fruity, with just a hint of dryness. Lorel drank rather more of the wine than was probably wise, but told herself that she needed something to bolster up her already frayed nerves. Finally she pushed away her empty plate; then she sat back and looked at Lewis.

'All right,' she said bluntly. 'What do you intend to do about me?'

'Perhaps we ought to go over a few basic facts first,' Lewis suggested. 'Firstly, you do realise that if you walk out of here, you haven't got anywhere to go? You can't remember which hotel you're staying in, and there isn't enough money in your bag to pay for more than a couple of nights at some other hotel.'

'You've been through my handbag?' she accused indignantly.

'Yes,' he agreed, without the slightest trace of compunction. 'Which brings us to the second point. I now have your passport. Until I give it back to you, you're going to find it very hard to go anywhere at all.'

'I'll go to the Consulate,' she threatened immediately. 'They'll sort this mess out for me. And when

they hear what's happened, you could find yourself
in serious trouble!'

Lewis smiled in a superior way which she found
totally infuriating.

'How could I possibly be in trouble?' he enquired
smoothly. 'I've done my very best to help someone
who got into difficulties. I've taken you into my house,
paid the doctor's bill, and made every effort to make
sure that you had the best possible treatment.'

'You've also accused me of being a thief, threatened
to keep me here against my will, and taken away my
passport,' she shot back at him furiously. 'I don't
think the Consulate would approve of that!'

Lewis was still smiling. 'Could you prove any of
those accusations?' he challenged her. 'I'd deny them,
of course. And Maria would be willing to swear that
you've been treated with nothing except kindness and
consideration during the time you've been at the
Palazzo Gregolino.'

'Kindness and consideration?' yelped Lorel. 'You
don't know the meaning of the words!'

'On the other hand,' went on Lewis, as if she hadn't
even spoken, 'you might not come out of it at all well.
Not after they find out that you're a thief. In fact,
when I tell them that you've stolen a briefcase con-
taining very valuable papers, you could even find
yourself facing police proceedings.'

For a moment, her blood actually ran cold. Then
a small grin appeared on her face. 'I might not be
able to prove that you tried to keep me a prisoner
here, but you've got exactly the same problem,' she
said triumphantly. '*You* can't prove that *I* took your
stupid briefcase!'

Lewis's expression didn't change. 'Oh, but I can,' he informed her softly. 'One of the passengers on the train saw you walking off with it. I have his name, the address of his hotel, and his assurance that he'll be willing to repeat that piece of information to the police, whenever I ask him to.'

The grin faded from Lorel's face. 'You're bluffing,' she muttered, but even she could hear the lack of conviction in her voice.

'Want to take that risk?' invited Lewis.

Lorel knew perfectly well that she didn't. What was the alternative, though? She gave a small shiver. She already knew the answer to that!

'I know I'm not a thief,' she stated very clearly, at last. 'But until I can remember those missing couple of days, I won't know exactly what happened, and who's telling the truth about all of this.' She looked at him with open hostility. 'If I agree to stay here at the *palazzo* for a while, what exactly would you expect me to do?'

'Whatever I ask of you,' he replied evenly.

Her eyes flew wide open. 'Oh, no! I'm not going along with anything like that.'

'It won't be anything too dreadful—or shocking,' Lewis mocked, obviously amused by her alarmed reaction. 'I simply want to keep you under the sort of conditions where you can get back the rest of your memory. In fact, all I want you to do is to rest and relax.'

'I still don't see why I have to stay *here*,' she said in annoyance.

'Where else could you go?' came his very reasonable reply.

Lorel pulled a face. She supposed he had a point there. 'How long do you intend to keep me here?' she asked.

'I've managed to postpone my business meetings for a few more days. If your memory isn't back by then, and we still haven't found the briefcase, then I'll have to rethink the situation.'

'My ticket back home is booked for the end of this week.'

'I'm sure the departure date can be changed.' Lewis got to his feet. 'You'd better take it easy for the rest of the day. The doctor's coming to give you a final check-up tomorrow morning.'

'More bills,' she muttered unhappily. 'It's going to take me for ever to pay you back.'

'I haven't asked for any repayment,' Lewis pointed out a little sharply.

Her head swiftly came up. 'Well, you're going to get it! I certainly don't intend to be in any kind of debt to you.'

Lewis shook his head irritably. 'You're a very difficult girl.'

'Then just let me leave,' she shot back immediately. 'That way, you won't have to be bothered with me any more.'

'No.' His tone was firm and final. 'Like it or not, you're staying here. In fact, I don't want you leaving the *palazzo* at all, not even for a walk, unless I come with you.'

'You *are* keeping me a prisoner!' she accused.

'Not really. You're free to walk out that door any time you please—as long as you're prepared to take the consequences.'

He left the room after that, leaving her to think about his last statement. It didn't take her too long. She was in a mess, and she knew it. Worse than that, she had no one she could turn to for help or advice. Too late, she wished she hadn't come on this holiday on her own. If she had waited until the summer, then she could have come with a couple of friends. But no, she'd had to rush off on the spur of the moment, and now she was definitely regretting it. Being in Venice on her own was no fun. On top of that, she was beginning to feel horribly vulnerable and alone, and it was an extremely unpleasant sensation.

She sighed deeply. If only she hadn't met Lewis Elliott. And the worst part was that she couldn't even remember meeting him! She knew it had happened on the train—at least, that was what he had told her, and she supposed he had no reason to lie about that— but the whole thing was a total blank as far as she was concerned. That put her at a serious disadvantage, and she was sure that was a very dangerous position to be in where Lewis Elliott was concerned.

The doctor came in the morning, and pronounced himself satisfied with her physical condition. At least, that was what she supposed he had said. She had to rely on Lewis's translation, and she began to wish that she understood more than a few very basic words of Italian.

For the rest of the day, she wandered rather restlessly around the *palazzo*, exploring its many rooms, gaping a little at its unashamed splendour, and wishing that circumstances had been different, so that she could have enjoyed her stay here.

In the afternoon, she spent a couple of hours with Maria, in the kitchen. Maria chattered almost non-stop and, although Lorel hadn't the faintest idea what she was saying, she felt relaxed with the big, friendly woman. More than than, she felt safe. She had the feeling that Lewis wouldn't dare to do anything out of line while Maria was around.

She joined Lewis in the large, formal dining-room for the evening meal. He didn't seem in a very talkative mood, which suited her fine. Since she still hadn't got back a single scrap of her missing chunk of memory, they really didn't have a lot to discuss.

Maria bustled in and out with plates, and a rather fierce look on her face. As she set the final course on the table, she said something in a severe undertone to Lewis, who hesitated for a moment, and then finally answered her. A fairly lengthy conversation followed, and Lorel got more and more frustrated at not being able to follow any of it.

Maria at last stalked out, pausing in the doorway to throw one final disapproving glare at Lewis, who calmly ignored it. As she closed the door very noisily behind her, Lorel looked at Lewis with some curiosity.

'What was that all about?'

'I've just turned down Maria's offer to stay at the *palazzo* overnight,' Lewis replied.

Lorel rather uneasily digested that piece of information. 'Then she doesn't live in?' she said at last, with a faintly worried wrinkling of her nose.

'No. She'll be leaving once she's cleared away the dishes.'

'Why did she want to stay?'

He raised one dark eyebrow. 'I'd have thought that fairly obvious. She still thinks you need a chaperone.'

'But you don't agree with her?'

Lewis's eyebrow inched a fraction higher. 'I think we can cope with the situation on our own, don't you?' he replied smoothly. Then his mouth curled into a cool smile. 'Of course, Maria didn't give in without a struggle,' he went on, in an amused tone. 'I had to promise her that I wouldn't lay a single finger on you. She does seem very worried about your virtue,' he added, and this time his voice had a faintly mocking undertone that she didn't understand.

'And do you usually keep your promises?' she asked cautiously.

His blue eyes gleamed. 'Not always.'

'That doesn't surprise me! Personally, I don't trust you an inch.'

His expression changed fractionally. 'You trusted me once.'

'When?' she demanded.

'On the ferry, when you were going through a bad patch because of your phobia about the sea. And then later, on the train, there was another time when you trusted me, let me——' His voice, which had taken on an unexpectedly husky note, abruptly broke off.

Lorel stared at him in irritation. Why was he waffling on about something that he knew she couldn't remember? She wished he would stop it. She didn't like the intense look that had come over his face. Or the way that his voice had suddenly changed.

'I've had enough to eat,' she cut in quickly, determined to change the subject. She got to her feet. 'I think I'll go outside for a while and get some fresh air.'

'It's cold out this evening,' Lewis told her. 'And it's starting to rain.'

She frowned in annoyance. 'Whenever I've seen pictures of Venice, it's always been basking in the sunshine.'

'Those pictures were probably taken in the summer,' Lewis commented. 'In spring, the weather's far more changeable. Heavy showers are quite common.' He also got up. 'Come and join me in the drawing-room for a while. I'll open another bottle of wine.'

'I don't want anything more to drink.'

'But I do.'

She studied him warily. That funny note was back in his voice again. He looked quite normal, though, and his eyes seemed quite cool, which she found re-assuring. In her albeit limited experience, men's eyes were a dead giveaway. When they became hot and overbright, it was definitely time to run!

The drawing-room was at the back of the *palazzo*, and large doors opened out on to a narrow terrace, with a flight of steps leading down to a small walled garden. In daylight, and with the sun shining, it must have been warm and peaceful. In the evening, with driving rain beating against the windows, it lost a lot of its charm.

Lewis pulled the heavy curtains, and then set about opening the bottle of wine.

'Want to change your mind and have some?' he asked, as he poured a glass for himself.

'Oh—all right,' she agreed. Perhaps getting slightly sloshed would help the evening to pass more quickly and pleasantly.

Lewis didn't sit down, but instead moved rather restlessly around the room. Lorel, who had slumped into an uncomfortable chair with tapestry cushions and thin, spindly legs, looked at him with a touch of irritation.

'Are you going to pace around like that all evening?'

'I should have gone to the first of those business meetings today,' growled Lewis. 'It's very inconvenient, having to postpone everything for a few days.'

'And I suppose it's all my fault?' she retorted.

'Of course it is. If you hadn't taken my damned briefcase——'

Lorel gave an exaggerated sigh. 'If you mention that briefcase one more time, I think I'll scream! It's just about your only topic of conversation. Are you always this boring?'

A dark expression swiftly spread over his features. 'If it's boring to have a certain sense of responsibility, then yes, I probably am! A lot of people's jobs depend on me running my company efficiently and profitably. If I can pull off these new contracts, then it'll mean more expansion—and more jobs. Maybe that all sounds very dull to you, but to someone who's unemployed, it would mean a great deal.'

'Yes, I can see that,' she grudgingly conceded.

'So, the sooner you get back the rest of your memory, the better it's going to be for everyone,' Lewis continued. 'You agree about that?'

'Of course. I just don't see how we're going to go about it. The doctor's prescription of rest and relaxation doesn't seem to be working.'

'There was something else he said we could try.'

She looked up at him cautiously. 'What?'

'Jogging your memory with familiar places and people.'

Lorel shrugged. 'I suppose it's worth a try. I haven't been in Venice long enough, though, to have gone to very many places.'

'You went to St Mark's square,' replied Lewis.

'Did I? Oh, yes,' she recalled. 'I remember you telling me that you'd seen me there, just before I had my fall. Well, I suppose we could go back to the square, and see if it rings any bells. As for people, though——' She gave a wry shake of her head. 'About the only person I seem to know in Venice is you, and you certainly haven't jogged any memories.'

'Perhaps that's because we haven't been doing the right things—going about it in the right way,' Lewis suggested softly.

She shot a sharp glance at him, wondering exactly what he was getting at. Then her nerves gave a brief twitch. His eyes weren't quite as cool as they had been earlier. Their vivid blue was a little deeper, a little brighter—and she found that distinctly worrying.

Rather hurriedly, she got to her feet and put down her half-finished glass of wine.

'Er—I feel a bit tired,' she muttered. 'I think I'll have an early night——'

She went to walk past him, but Lewis laid one hand on her arm, easily detaining her.

'None of this seems at all familiar?' he suggested. 'Eating a meal together, talking, having a little too much to drink?'

'Definitely not!' she said firmly. 'I'm sure we haven't done any of this before.'

'No?'

That single word seemed to hang in the air between them for an awfully long time. Then Lewis shifted his position slightly, moving a few inches closer.

'And how about this?' he murmured. 'Do you think we could possibly have done this before?'

For the very briefest of moments, there *was* something about that hot blue gaze that seemed frighteningly familiar. Then the feeling vanished, and she braced herself for the kiss that she was quite certain was going to follow. When it came, though, it was little more than the lightest brushing of his lips against her own. Then Lewis reached up and twined one of her gold-brown curls around his finger.

'Nice hair,' he said appreciatively. 'A pretty colour, and soft to the touch.'

'Thank you,' she said stiffly. 'Is that all? Can I go now?'

He seemed to consider her question. 'No, I don't think so,' he said at last. 'First of all, I think you should try touching me.'

'What?' she squeaked.

Lewis's mouth relaxed into a slow smile. 'I'm not suggesting anything too intimate. Remember, I promised Maria that I'd behave like a gentleman! Just try touching my arm, or perhaps my shoulder.'

Lorel blinked at him. 'Why?'

'Never mind the questions for now. Just do it,' he ordered.

And somehow, it was very difficult to refuse him when he used that particular tone of voice. Edgily, Lorel reached up and let her hand rest briefly on his forearm. She could feel the firm muscles beneath the fine material of his suit, and she let go of him again fairly quickly. Something about the feel of his body definitely disturbed her.

'Nothing?' enquired Lewis. 'No reaction at all?'

'Of course not,' she said at once, although not altogether truthfully. 'What did you think was going to happen?'

He shrugged. 'Nothing, really. I suppose it was just a shot in the dark. Still, perhaps I ought to try just one more time——'

And this time he kissed her extremely thoroughly. Since she hadn't been expecting it, he caught her totally off guard. Without even thinking what she was doing, she opened her mouth to him, and then silently gasped as he instantly took advantage of her unexpected submission.

Realising too late what was happening, she tried to twist away, but he wouldn't let her. Nor would he release her mouth. His tongue relentlessly probed and teased, and to her horror she found his hands were beginning to do the same. What was worse, he was behaving as if he were perfectly familiar with what his restless fingers were exploring. It was as if he felt he had every *right* to be touching her with this devastating intimacy.

She tried to protest, but couldn't. He wouldn't let her. One touch from him stifled the words in her throat, and small rivulets of sweat and pleasure twined together and ran down her body. She began to shake, not understanding what was happening. And her head felt funny, as if a door somewhere inside it had just opened a fraction. She wanted to push it hard and see right through it, but something stopped her. Perhaps she was simply frightened of seeing what lay on the other side, she reasoned with herself dazedly.

Lewis's mouth finally eased its pressure, and his hand came to rest under the swell of her breast. Only one finger moved now, slowly stroking her soft flesh, but even that was enough to make her gulp.

'You—you shouldn't be doing this,' she got out unsteadily.

'Why not?'

His voice was calm, in stark contrast to his eyes, which told her something else entirely.

Lorel swallowed hard. 'You promised Maria you'd behave like a gentleman.'

'Promises like that were made to be broken,' he said disconcertingly. His hand shifted with sudden impatience. His palm grazed the aching tip of her breast, and she heard his breath catch at the same time as her own.

'I've never behaved like this with a woman before,' he told her huskily. 'Never had this urge to simply take what I want. Or would it be taking?' he questioned softly, his blue eyes blazing down into her own. 'Perhaps you'd give it to me quite willingly?'

She was alarmed to find his suggestion didn't shock her nearly as much as it should have. She briefly closed her eyes, and fervently wished he would remove his hand. How on earth could she think straight when he was setting off those small starbursts of pleasure inside her?

Almost as if he could read her thoughts, he let go of her. Although she had thought it was what she wanted, she felt oddly disappointed and empty once he had moved away from her. She also had the feeling that he had found it quite an effort to release her, and for some reason that pleased her.

Lewis kept his back to her for a few moments. When he finally turned back to face her, his eyes were much calmer, and he seemed very much in control of himself again.

'None of this has turned out quite the way I expected,' he said drily. Lorel had the feeling that the faint note of mockery in his voice was aimed at himself, not her. 'And since kisses won't jog your memory, then tomorrow we'd better try something else.'

Confused and disturbed, she gazed back at him. 'Why should kisses jog my memory?' she asked shakily, not very sure that she even wanted to know the answer to her question.

'Until you get your memory back, you won't know, will you?' he replied, his face quite unreadable now. He turned away from her. 'Goodnight, Lorel. And I hope you'll sleep better than I'm going to tonight!'

With that, he rather abruptly left the drawing-room. Lorel shivered as she sat down in the nearest chair. The more time she spent with Lewis Elliott, the less she understood him. And now this had happened . . .

It was disturbing, to say the least. And perhaps the most unnerving part of the whole affair was that it hadn't felt strange, it hadn't felt wrong. In fact, it was almost as if it had happened before.

At that, Lorel raised her head with some determination. That was nonsense! There was no way she could have got herself involved with a man like Lewis Elliott. Anyway, they had only been together on that train for a matter of hours. Nothing could have happened in that time! And there was an obvious explanation for tonight. They had both had a little too much wine, and got rather stupidly carried away.

Glad to have sorted everything out so satisfactorily, she got to her feet and took herself off to bed. And, though she didn't sleep too well, she managed to convince herself that it had absolutely nothing to do with the events of the evening.

CHAPTER SIX

LOREL got up the next morning not knowing quite what to expect. The events of last night were still uncomfortably clear in her mind, and she had a distinctly nervous feeling in her stomach as she made her way downstairs.

The rain of yesterday evening had cleared away, and it was another of those bright, golden days which seemed to touch Venice with a particular magic that was all its own. Lorel wasn't in a mood to appreciate it, though. Instead, she prowled around restlessly, waiting for Lewis to make an appearance, and wondering what he was going to say—or do—when he did finally show up.

When the door eventually opened, though, it was only Maria, bringing in hot coffee and croissants. She gave Lorel a searching look, as if wanting to reassure herself that no harm had befallen her since yesterday evening. Then she smiled at her, and launched into a flood of Italian, to which Lorel replied with a rather inadequate, *'Buon giorno.'*

After Maria had left, Lorel spread marmalade on one of the croissants, and nibbled at it unenthusiastically. Then the door opened again, and this time it was Lewis who walked in.

The piece of croissant in Lorel's mouth immediately seemed as large as a loaf of bread. Somehow, she managed to swallow it, and gulped down a couple of mouthfuls of coffee to help it down her dry throat.

113

'Er—hello,' she said rather weakly.

She was annoyed that she was behaving in this feeble way—after all, he hadn't done much more than kiss her last night—but for some reason she couldn't seem to help it. And, to add to her irritation, Lewis himself looked very relaxed this morning. No sign of twitchiness on *his* part.

'Have you got any plans for today?' he asked, helping himself to some coffee.

'No,' she replied, her tone slightly wary now. 'Why?'

'I thought we might go for a walk.'

'A walk?' she echoed, looking at him wide-eyed.

Amusement briefly showed in Lewis's eyes. 'There's nothing particularly outrageous about that suggestion, is there?'

'Well—no.'

'Then why are you looking at me as if I'd just invited you to spend a week in bed?'

A fresh wave of flustered confusion swept over her. 'I'm not—I'm sure you wouldn't—I mean—— Thoroughly irritated with herself, she shook her head. 'Damn it, I wish you'd stop doing this to me!'

'Doing what?' he enquired innocently.

She shot a black glance at him. 'You know perfectly well!'

He looked at her with laughing eyes. 'So that kiss last night *did* get to you.'

'It certainly did not,' she retorted. 'It was just a kiss, that was all. Nothing special.'

'Mmm.' From his tone, it was very clear that he didn't believe her. Conceited pig! she thought furiously to herself.

'If that kiss was as marvellous as you obviously thought it was, then why didn't it bring back my memory?' she challenged him. 'After all, that was what it was meant to do, wasn't it?'

'I can't quite remember the reason for it,' Lewis said cheerfully. 'But I *do* remember exactly how it felt,' he added in a much softer tone.

A small shiver curled its way down Lorel's spine. So did she! She was determined not to let herself think about it too much, though. She was sure it wouldn't be at all sensible.

'What about this walk?' she said, determined to change the subject. 'Where were you planning on going?'

'To St Mark's Square,' he told her. 'I thought you might like to come along, and see if anything looks familiar.'

'Still trying to jog my memory?'

Lewis shrugged. 'It seems worth a try. It's the one place in Venice that I know you've visited. Going back there might just make something click inside your head.'

'And when it comes down to it, that's all you really care about, isn't it?' she said with some annoyance. 'Making me remember where I put your rotten briefcase!'

His eyes remained steady. 'Occasionally, I have other things on my mind.'

Lorel decided that she didn't want to know what those 'other things' were.

'All right, I'll come with you,' she agreed rather hastily. 'It's a lovely morning, and I could do with some fresh air.'

She went up to fetch a light jacket. It felt rather odd to be clothed from head to foot in things which Lewis had bought for her, but she was sensible enough to know that she didn't have much alternative except to wear them.

When she came down again, she found Lewis waiting for her in the high-ceilinged entrance hall. Her gaze slid over his immaculate shirt and obviously expensive suit.

'You're always dressed so formally,' she commented. 'Don't you ever relax? You're meant to be on holiday.'

'Perhaps I need someone to teach me how to unwind,' he suggested smoothly.

Lorel caught the glint in his eyes, and decided she definitely *wasn't* going to volunteer.

Lewis gave her a sideways smile, and then swung open the heavy front door. 'Ready?' he asked.

She nodded, and they stepped out into the sunshine.

Lewis led the way confidently through the maze of narrow streets and alleyways. Lorel was completely lost after the first couple of twists and turns, and she just hoped that he really did know where he was going. She knew that most men would never admit that they were lost, even if they didn't have the slightest idea where they were. It dented their macho image, she supposed.

They crossed a small bridge over one of the side canals, and Lorel paused in the middle for a few moments, peering over the edge to the murky water below.

'The canals look a lot more romantic from a distance,' she said a trifle ruefully, gazing down at the rubbish floating on the water. 'They smell a lot better, too!'

'It's far worse in summer, when it gets really hot,' Lewis remarked. Then, as she went to cross the rest of the bridge, he added, 'Mind the steps.'

She negotiated them carefully, and then realised that Lewis was watching her with a rather intent expression on his face.

'What is it?' she asked curiously.

'This is where you fell and hit your head,' he told her.

'Here?' She looked around in surprise; then she stared up at the surrounding buildings with their faded splendour, peeling paintwork, and narrow, wrought-iron balconies. 'Sorry,' she said, with a small shrug. 'None of this seems in the least familiar. I really don't remember being here before.' Then she frowned. 'What was I doing here, anyway? It seems quite a way from any of the main tourist spots.' When Lewis didn't answer immediately, she added half to herself, 'Perhaps I got lost. I haven't got much of a sense of direction.'

'Perhaps you did,' he said, in what seemed to her to be an unnecessarily curt voice. Then he gave a slightly frustrated gesture with his hands. 'If none of this means anything to you, we'd better move on.'

'I'm *trying* to remember,' Lorel said apologetically. 'But it's no good, there's just nothing there.'

Lewis looked as if he didn't entirely believe her. Lorel scowled at his back as he turned away from her. Did he still think she was faking the amnesia? Surely he didn't really believe she would do something as stupid as that?

She gave a brief sigh, and then trudged after him
as he strode on ahead. Lewis Elliott was a very difficult—in fact, an impossible—man to fathom out.
She didn't understand the reasons for most things he
did, and had absolutely no idea what his true feelings
towards her were. More often than not, he gave the
impression that he found her nothing more than a
nuisance, someone who had come charging into his
life and disrupted it in a way that he found distinctly
irritating. Other times, she wasn't quite so sure. He
had developed the habit of looking at her in a manner
that made her nerves curl rather pleasantly. And, of
course, there had been that kiss last night . . .

Lewis suddenly turned round and looked at her at
that point. Lorel instantly felt her cheeks grow uncomfortably hot. He couldn't possibly know she had
been thinking about that kiss, she argued with herself.
He wasn't a mind-reader!

All the same, he seemed to be studying her very
intently. Lorel stared back at him rather crossly. Being
under such close scrutiny made her feel distinctly edgy,
and she didn't like it.

To her relief, he released her from that blue gaze
only a few seconds later.

'We're getting near St Mark's Square now,' he told
her.

She could have guessed that, because the narrow
streets were beginning to fill up with people. They
walked on, and after turning a couple more corners,
the square lay in front of them, basking in the spring
sunshine and filled with people and pigeons.

Lorel let her gaze slide over the familiar land-
marks: the belltower, the Basilica of St Mark's, and
the huge square itself. Then she sighed. It was only

amiliar because she had seen so many pictures of it.
She certainly couldn't remember being here in person.

'You don't remember going to the top of the bell-
ower?' queried Lewis. 'Or sightseeing inside the
Basilica?'

Lorel shook her head. 'No,' she said gloomily.

Lewis gave a brief frown. 'I suppose that now we're
here, we may as well stay a little longer. Let's go and
have a cup of coffee.'

He steered her towards one of the tables set outside
he cafés that lined the square. When the coffee ar-
ived, Lorel slowly sipped it, feeling unexpectedly
depressed.

'What were you expecting?' asked Lewis percep-
ively. 'A sudden bolt of lightning inside your head,
and all the missing pieces tumbling right back into
place?'

'I suppose so,' she admitted.

'Stop thinking about it,' he advised. 'Just let it come
back naturally. You'll probably remember everything
when you're least expecting it.'

'That's an odd piece of advice, coming from you!'
he retorted. '*You're* the one who's so anxious for me
o remember everything. That's why we're here, isn't
t? Because you thought it might jolt my memory if
you brought me to a familiar place?'

He didn't answer straight away. 'This morning, it
doesn't seem quite so important,' he said at last, in
an unexpectedly quiet voice.

She looked at him in surprise. 'Why not? Don't
you want to know what I did with your briefcase?'

One of his eyebrows lifted. 'Then you're willing to
accept that you did steal it?'

'Certainly not,' she said with some determination, angry at the way she had let him lead her into that admission. 'I'm just pointing out that you seem to have changed your tune.'

'It's probably only temporary,' he said with a smile. 'Put it down to the fact that it's a beautiful morning, and I'm feeling good about certain things.'

Lorel looked at him suspiciously. 'What sort of things?'

He gazed back at her calmly. 'Maybe that kiss last night is one of them,' he suggested.

Uneasiness spread through her stomach. To try and hide it, she put on her most blasé expression.

'I'm surprised you still remember it. I'd forgotten about it, until you mentioned it.'

This time, he actually laughed out loud. 'Lorel Parker, you are an extremely bad liar,' he said at last, still grinning broadly. 'You remember it as well as I do. Perhaps even better,' he added, his eyes positively gleaming now. As the colour flared brightly in her face again, he sat back and continued to look at her with great amusement. 'All right, if you don't want to talk about it, we'll change the subject. Why did you take your holiday so early in the year? Wouldn't it have been more fun for you if you'd waited until the summer, and come with some friends?'

'I really felt as if I needed the break,' she explained, glad of the opportunity to talk about something else. 'I didn't want to wait a couple more months. Then that legacy from my great-aunt arrived out of the blue, and I decided to blow the lot on a luxury holiday, to cheer myself up. Travelling on the Orient-Express seemed about as luxurious as you could get, and I thought I'd probably be able to make friends with people of my own age once I got to Venice.'

'Why did you need cheering up?' asked Lewis. 'Or had it something to do with the death of your parents?' he went on perceptively.

Lorel wrinkled her nose. 'I'd forgotten I'd told you about that.' She twisted her fingers together a little restlessly. 'You don't really want to hear about it, do you? It's a fairly long and dull story.'

'Try me,' he invited.

She gave a faint sigh. 'Well—first of all, I suppose you've got to understand what my parents were like. They were—very frivolous,' she said with some reluctance, not particularly eager to talk about such a private and personal subject. 'They thought life was one long round of parties and fun. They never took anything seriously.'

'Is that such a bad way to be?' suggested Lewis, much to her surprise.

'I didn't think you'd approve of that sort of attitude to life!'

'Everyone has to find their own way of getting through each day.'

This time, her eyebrows really did shoot up. 'Are you trying to tell me that you find life boring?'

Lewis lifted his shoulders non-committally. 'Sometimes, it does seem to be all work, with very little time for relaxation or pleasure.'

'The stresses of being a top executive?' she said drily. 'Come on, surely it's got its compensations. All that power—and money!'

'You think they're important?'

Something in his tone puzzled her. 'No,' she said, after a moment's hesitation. 'But a lot of people do.'

'And you think I'm one of them?'

Lorel decided she didn't want to get any deeper into this. 'I don't know you well enough to make that sort of judgement,' she said firmly.

'No?' Then he seemed to decide that he, too, had said more than enough on the subject. 'How did we get side-tracked like this?' he said, much more briskly. 'We were talking about your parents, and their approach to life. How did you fit into all their non-stop partying and relentless fun?'

'Not very well,' she admitted. 'Don't get the wrong impression,' she added quickly. 'They certainly loved me, in their own way. I don't think it was their fault that I couldn't seem to fit in.'

'Did you have a lonely sort of childhood?' asked Lewis.

'No, not really. Even when my parents had sloped off somewhere, there were always lots of other people around to look after me. My parents kept a sort of open house. Their friends were coming and going all the time, and they were all pretty fond of me. I was never left on my own, and I certainly wasn't unhappy. I just felt—well, sort of out of place. I tried to fit in, but I couldn't seem to manage it. I think I was born conventional,' she added wryly.

'Conventional?' repeated Lewis, with obvious disbelief. 'From my experience of you, that's about the last word I'd use to describe you!'

'Well, I might have acted out of character these last few days, but that's really the way I am. At least, compared with my parents,' she said, with a grimace. 'But I suppose anyone would seem a bit staid, next to them.'

'Did it hit you hard when they died?'

'Yes. It was like a great black hole in my life. I never thought I'd miss anyone so much. And it changed my whole life in a way that I hadn't expected.'

'How?' asked Lewis with interest.

'I blamed the way they died on the way that they lived,' she explained. Seeing his slightly puzzled look, she went on, 'They were always rushing off and doing things on the spur of the moment. They'd get together with a few friends, someone would suggest a party, a trip to the coast, a couple of days away somewhere, and they'd be up and off without even thinking about it. I know *exactly* what happened on the day they died. The sea was rough, and the forecast was for the weather to get even worse. When someone suggested a few hours' sailing, though, they didn't even stop to think about it. They piled into the boat with a couple of their friends, sailed off without giving a thought to even simple safety precautions—and drowned.'

Even now, she couldn't quite keep the bitterness out of her voice.

'You think their deaths could have been prevented?' said Lewis quietly.

'I know they could! If they had just behaved responsibly for once in their lives——' She broke off rather abruptly. She couldn't seem to say anything else, not at the moment.

'Do you want some more coffee?'

She shook her head.

'Then how about something stronger?'

'No, thanks,' she muttered, finding her voice again.

Lewis sat back. 'How did all of this change *your* life?'

'I decided I didn't want to be like them in any way, I didn't want to live the way they had. I suppose it was a kind of backlash reaction,' she admitted. 'The trouble was, I took it to extremes. Until then, I'd rather flitted around from job to job. I'd done some modelling, worked in local radio for a while, even got involved with a pop group for a few months, although that didn't really come to anything. Probably because I'm a lousy singer,' she admitted, with a wry smile. 'None of it offered any long-term career prospects, of course, but my parents were always encouraging me to try something different, and telling me I should only take jobs that seemed like fun. I didn't know if it was what *I* wanted or not, but I went along with it. I suppose I was trying to please them, and still making some kind of effort to fit in with their own sort of life-style. After they died, though, I chucked all that in and went to business college for a year. Then, when I'd got some basic qualifications, I took a job with a firm of accountants.'

'You certainly couldn't get much more staid than that,' Lewis commented drily. 'My guess is that it wasn't much fun, though.'

'No fun at all,' she admitted. 'Looking back, I can see that I rather went over the top. I hardly ever went out anywhere, I lost touch with most of my friends, and I put all my energy into work. I must have been the ideal employee!'

'What made you change?'

She lifted her shoulders in a rueful gesture. 'I don't really know. I just woke up one morning and thought how ridiculous the whole thing was. I was twenty-three years old, and behaving as if I were already middle-aged. My life was totally dull, and I could see it wasn't going to change unless I made a real effort. When that small legacy from my great-aunt turned up so unexpectedly, I realised it was a great chance to haul myself out of the rut I'd dug myself into. I chucked in my job, booked a luxury holiday, and high-tailed it off here, to Venice.' She gave a faint grin. 'I suppose it wasn't a very wise thing to do, but at least the last few days haven't been dull. At least,' she amended, 'the ones that I can remember haven't been! Until I get back the rest of my memory, I won't know about the rest.'

She was a little surprised to find that Lewis wasn't smiling back at her. In fact, his face had gone rather dark, as if he were thinking about something that didn't particularly please him.

'You realise that you may never get your memory back?' he said rather abruptly.

Lorel blinked. 'Did the doctor say that was likely?'

'Not in so many words. You've got to face the fact that it's a possibility, though.'

'That would be very inconvenient for you,' she pointed out.

'Would it?' he replied, rather enigmatically.

'Well, of course! You wouldn't get your briefcase back.'

'Forget about the damned briefcase for a while!'

His unexpectedly terse reply made her shake her head in bewilderment. 'I don't understand you. For the last few days, practically all you've talked about is that briefcase. Now you're behaving as if it isn't even important.'

Lewis growled something under his breath; then he signalled to the waiter to bring more coffee. Lorel could see that she wasn't going to get any explanation out of him for his odd behaviour. She gave a slightly impatient sigh, and then turned her head away from him, watching instead the crowds of people who were either standing around admiring the views, or feeding the pigeons that massed in the square, looking for titbits.

When she finally looked back at Lewis again, she found his blue gaze was now fixed on her with unswerving intensity. She had the feeling that he had been studying her like that for quite some time and, for some reason, it made her skin prickle.

'You keep staring at me today as if I've got two heads!' she said irritably. 'I wish you would stop it.'

The dark expression disappeared from his face, and in its place came a more familiar bland look.

'I do apologise,' he said a little mockingly. 'In future, I'll only look at you when I'm actually talking to you.'

'Don't be silly,' she muttered. 'I just meant——'

'Meant what?'

But Lorel didn't want to go into it any deeper. She didn't have the faintest idea why it so unsettled her when Lewis looked at her in a certain way, and she certainly didn't know why it made her legs feel uncomfortably weak.

'We've spent practically the whole morning talking about my family,' she said, deciding it was definitely time to get on to another subject. 'How about telling me something about yours?'

'What do you want to know?'

'Everything,' she said promptly. 'Do you realise that I know hardly anything about you, except for your name?'

'I told you quite a few details on the train.'

'Well, that's not much good, since I can't remember them. You'd better tell me all over again.'

With a small shrug, he began to talk about his company, Elliott Communications. Lorel listened carefully, but none of it seemed familiar. It was as if she were hearing it for the first time.

'Do you enjoy your job?' she asked at last. Then she pulled a face. 'I suppose that's rather a silly question. You wouldn't be doing it otherwise. Anyway, I should think that most men would give their right arm for the sort of position you've got.'

'Maybe. I didn't have much choice, though. When my father died suddenly, I had to take over the company.'

'Didn't you want to take it over?' she asked, surprised.

He didn't answer straight away. 'It was what I was trained for, what it was always assumed I would do,' he said at last. 'My father would have hated it if an outsider had been brought in to run the company, after he had gone. I don't actually dislike my job, and I do it well. But I sometimes think——'

'Think what?' she asked curiously.

'That it would have been nice to have had a choice.'

'You could have just told your father that you had other plans for your life,' Lorel said bluntly. 'I'm sure he would have understood.'

'I dare say he would,' agreed Lewis. 'But that wouldn't have made it any less painful for him. He was always obsessed with the idea of handing the company down from father to son.'

'You can't make your own life miserable because of someone else's obsession.'

'Didn't you tell me only minutes ago that you took jobs you didn't really want, because you thought it would please your parents?' he reminded her.

'Yes, but——' She frowned briefly. 'It's not the same—is it?' she finished uncertainly.

'It seems exactly the same to me,' replied Lewis. His gaze held hers steadily. 'Perhaps we've more in common than we realised.'

Lorel fiddled with a spoon. 'Perhaps,' she said finally, and with some reluctance. She glanced up at Lewis, and found his eyes were gleaming. 'No, I don't think you're right about that at all,' she contradicted herself rather crossly. 'I'm sure we haven't got *anything* in common.'

'You don't like the idea of sharing—certain things with me?' he suggested smoothly.

'I just don't think we're alike,' she insisted firmly. 'Anyway, stop trying to change the subject, and tell me more about your family. Haven't you got any brothers who could have taken over the company, instead of you?'

'There's only my stepbrother, Felix. And I don't think he's ever done a serious day's work in his life.' Lewis paused, then went on in a darker tone, 'Strictly speaking, I don't actually have any real family. My mother died shortly after I was born, and my father remarried a few years later. Now that he's dead, I'm left with a stepmother, a stepbrother, and a stepsister.'

Something in his tone clearly told her that he wasn't overly fond of this new family he had acquired.

'You don't get on with them?'

'Katie—my stepsister—is the best of the bunch. She's bright and clever, and we've always got along well. She got married recently, though, so she doesn't

live at home any more. Felix, my stepbrother——'
Lewis's brows drew together in a gathering frown.
'Felix is extremely charming—and a complete pain in
the backside. I don't think he even knows the meaning
of the word "responsibility". I seem to have spent
half my life—and heaven knows how much money—
getting him out of one mess after the other.'

'What about your stepmother?'

Lewis's frown deepened, until it furrowed dark lines
into his forehead. 'My stepmother is the reason that
I don't go home very often. She spends my money,
interferes in my life, and generally drives me mad.
The house she's living in is mine, but she runs it as
if it were her own.'

'Why not just kick her out?' Lorel asked practically.

'Because I promised my father, just before he died,
that I'd take care of them all. Katie, Felix, and Rita,
my stepmother. Hell, the times I've regretted that
promise!' he went on darkly. 'Katie was never any
problem, I'd have looked after her for the rest of her
life, if that was what she had wanted. She was always
very independent, though. The only thing she would
ever take from me was an occasional word of advice!
Not like those other two leeches,' he added, his features lapsing back into a scowl. 'I sometimes think
they're going to be sucking the blood out of me until
the day I die!'

Lorel looked at him with growing fascination. She
seemed to be seeing him in a whole new and different
way. Not some all-powerful executive, zipping round
the world, making important decisions all day—and
a lot of money—but someone a lot more human. A
man who was doing a job he hadn't chosen for

himself, and at the same time supporting a thankless stepmother and stepbrother.

Lewis pushed his empty coffee-cup to one side. 'Let's go,' he said briefly. 'I've done enough talking for one morning.'

She wished she could ask him more, but knew she wouldn't get any more information out of him. She had the feeling that he very rarely opened up like this, talking about his personal life with such frankness. She had no idea why he had talked to her, but found that she was glad that he had.

'Are you going back to the *palazzo*?' she asked, picking her way carefully through the mass of pigeons that were waddling around in front of them.

'Yes. Do you want to stay on here, and do some sightseeing?'

Although she wasn't sure why, that idea didn't appeal to her.

'I think I'll come with you, if you don't mind.'

'Would you like to go in a gondola?' he offered, as casually as he might have suggested taking a bus.

'They're very expensive,' she said doubtfully.

For the first time in quite a while, a glint of amusement returned to Lewis's eyes. 'You think I can't afford it?'

'Oh, I'm sure that you can. But we could quite easily get the *vaporetto*.'

His eyes deepened a shade, in that disconcerting way they had of doing. 'But it wouldn't be nearly as romantic.'

There didn't seem a lot she could say to that. In fact, she wasn't sure that there was anything she *wanted* to say.

'All right, then,' she agreed, with a rather feeble shrug of resignation. 'A gondola it is.'

They made their way towards the Grand Canal which, as always, seemed packed with boats.

'Perhaps there won't be one free——' Lorel began. Then she noticed a gondola smoothly pulling into a nearby landing-stage, in response to a signal from Lewis. She briefly scowled. He was probably the sort of man who could whistle up a taxi from nowhere in the middle of London's rush hour!

She supposed the boat was stable enough, although it looked perilously long and thin. Just as Lewis was about to hand her down into it, though, he paused for a moment and shot her a quick look.

'I forgot you had a phobia about water. Will you be all right? You don't have to go ahead with this, if you don't want to.'

'I'll be fine,' she assured him. 'It's only the open sea that causes me real problems.'

She settled herself gingerly into one of the seats, and Lewis slid easily down beside her. There wasn't a lot of room but, even so, she didn't think his thigh needed to be pressed *quite* so closely against her own. He wasn't making any effort to move, though, and she didn't want to wriggle away in case she upset the boat. Even the smallest movement seemed to make it rock fairly alarmingly, and she clenched her fingers together nervously and told herself everything was going to be fine. She was going to *enjoy* this trip.

The gondolier was standing behind them, using the large, single-bladed oar to manoeuvre the boat away from the bank of the canal.

'Is he going to sing?' enquired Lorel.

'Not unless we pay him extra,' Lewis replied drily. 'Do you want to be serenaded?'

'No, thanks,' she said promptly. 'I think I'll just sit back and enjoy the views!'

Their progress down the Grand Canal was slow, compared to the motor-boats that whizzed past them, but it gave Lorel plenty of time to soak up the marvellous panorama that stretched out ahead of them. She gazed admiringly at the *palazzos*, some of them now converted into hotels, while others remained private residences. The bright spring sunshine showed their arched windows, decorative balconies and fine façades off to their best advantage, and even those that were in a state of disrepair still looked incredibly romantic.

They finally left the Grand Canal, and began to make their way along one of the smaller side canals. The gondola slid under a couple of arched bridges, and the houses that loomed up on either side weren't quite so picturesque, but still had bags of charm.

'This is great,' said Lorel with some satisfaction. 'I suppose that everyone who comes to Venice ought to take a trip in a gondola. If you can afford it, that is,' she added, a trifle wryly.

Lewis looked at her assessingly. 'Does my money worry you?' he asked unexpectedly.

Since she hadn't been expecting that question, she floundered for a few moments.

'No—of course not. I mean—well—it's actually nothing to do with me, is it? I don't *have* to worry about it.'

When he didn't answer her, she shot a wary glance at him. What was this all about? His face was quite unreadable, though. Lorel waited for him to say something more, but he remained silent. Eventually, she gave a small shrug and settled back to enjoy the views again.

She was quite sorry when they at last arrived back at the Palazzo Gregolino. The gondolier tied the boat to the thick, striped pole in front of the *palazzo*, and Lorel carefully clambered out of the boat. Then, with even more care, she negotiated the flight of crumbling steps that led up to the *palazzo*.

Lewis followed closely behind—in fact, he was a little *too* close, Lorel decided, with a touch of irritation. It always made her feel edgy when he began to physically crowd her like that. As soon as they set foot inside the *palazzo*, though, Maria came bustling out to meet them. She began to chatter rapidly to Lewis, who seemed to have no problem following her excited spate of Italian. With her message finally delivered, and having answered the couple of brief questions Lewis put to her, Maria returned to the kitchen.

Lorel looked at Lewis. 'What was that all about?'

'I thought your hotel might eventually contact the police when you didn't return to your room for several days, so I left a message with the local police, letting them know that you were staying here. They promised to get in touch if they had any word from the hotel.'

'And that's what has happened?' she asked.

'Yes. The hotel's finally reported you as missing.'

'So you know now where I'm staying? Good,' she said, with a pleased smile. 'That means I can get my own clothes back.'

Lewis's eyes had grown very cool. 'It also means something else,' he told her in an even tone. 'When we go round to your hotel room, I intend to search it thoroughly, to see if my missing briefcase is there. We're finally going to find out if you're a thief or not, Lorel Parker!'

CHAPTER SEVEN

THIS time, they didn't go in one of the elegant, leisurely-paced gondolas, but in a water-taxi. The motorboat whizzed them through the canals, and in a fairly short time deposited them at a landing-stage on one of the much smaller back canals.

'Is this where I was staying?' asked Lorel, looking up at the decidedly dilapidated hotel.

'This is the hotel which reported that a Miss Lorel Parker seemed to have gone missing.'

Lewis's tone was so neutral that she didn't have the slightest idea what was going through his head at the moment. Not that there was anything new in that. Lewis Elliott was a very hard man to figure out!

Lewis headed straight towards the entrance, but Lorel dawdled a little way behind him. Now that she was here, she was suddenly very reluctant to go in. Something inside her seemed to be afraid of what they might find there.

Come on, she told herself impatiently. Don't be such a coward! You're not scared of remembering those lost couple of days, are you?

She walked firmly into the reception area, and then looked around, trying hard to recognise the shabby surroundings. None of it seemed in the least familiar, though. She might have been setting foot in here for the first time.

Lewis was already talking to a middle-aged woman behind the desk. Then he nodded, took something from her, and came over to Lorel.

'She says you had a room on the first floor. She's given me the key.'

'Well, I suppose we'd better go up there,' she said, hoping he couldn't hear the nervous tremor that had somehow found its way into her voice.

They climbed the stairs in silence. When they reached the door, Lewis inserted the key in the lock, and opened it.

The room turned out to be small, but neat and clean, and it had a rather nice view from the window. Lorel looked round; then she turned back to Lewis, who had been watching her rather closely.

'Does any of this ring any bells with you?' he asked.

She shook her head. 'Absolutely none,' she said gloomily. 'I don't think that *anything's* going to bring back that lost bit of memory.'

He shrugged. 'I suppose it doesn't really matter, as long as I find my briefcase.'

'What do you mean, it doesn't matter?' demanded Lorel, with a sudden flash of pure anger. 'It sure as hell matters to me!' Then, as he opened the nearest wardrobe, and began rummaging through the contents, she added indignantly, 'And what do you think you're doing? Those are my things you're turning over.'

'How do you know that?' replied Lewis coolly. 'You can't remember if they're yours or not.'

'If this is my hotel room, then they've got to be mine. Stop treating them as if they're just jumble!'

Lewis straightened up. 'There's no need to get so uptight about it. Anyway, I don't need to look any further. I've found what I was after.'

Lorel's gaze slid down to his left hand; then she swallowed hard. He was holding a small black leather briefcase, which had his initials stamped on it in gold.

'Er—I wonder how that could possibly have got into my room,' she said rather feebly.

His blue gaze rested on her in a way that she definitely didn't like.

'It's here because you stole it,' he replied calmly.

She opened her mouth to protest, but then closed it again. She could hardly go on denying it when the evidence was there, right in front of her eyes!

'All right,' she muttered at last, 'I suppose I must have taken it.' She raised her head, and flung a fresh look of defiance at him. 'But if I did, then I want to know *why*. I must have had a very good reason.'

Lewis's own face altered. An expression swept across it that she just couldn't fathom at all.

'Perhaps you decided that you didn't like me very much,' he suggested in an even tone. 'Maybe you wanted to get back at me in some way.'

'Then what did you do to make me dislike you so much that I stole your case?' she demanded. She shook her head in frustration. 'You *know*, don't you? And all I can do is guess, because you won't tell me a damn thing!'

'Some things are best forgotten,' Lewis replied briefly. Then, before she could ask him exactly what he meant by that, he moved to the door. 'You'd better get your things together,' he instructed. 'I'll wait for you below, in reception. When you're ready, we'll go back to the *palazzo*.'

'And what if I prefer to stay here? After all, this *is* my hotel room. If I'm to stay anywhere in Venice, it should be here.'

He raised one eyebrow. 'Can you pay for it?'

'I don't have to, I booked it for a week——' Lorel began. Then her voice trailed away. That week was already more than up, and she certainly couldn't afford to book another.

'The way I see it, you don't have much choice except to return to the *palazzo*,' Lewis pointed out.

'Of course I have a choice! I can go back home, to England,' she declared, determined that this irritating man wasn't going to make all her decisions for her.

'Your return ticket is out of date,' he reminded her. 'Getting a refund, or re-booking it for a future date, could take some time. You'll need somewhere to stay while you get it sorted out.'

'And you're kindly offering to let me stay at the *palazzo*?' she enquired acidly.

'Yes, I am.'

'And what do you expect to get from me in return?'

Lewis's gaze froze to a very icy shade of blue. 'What exactly do you mean by that?'

'I'd have thought it was perfectly clear,' retorted Lorel. 'You took me in after my fall, paid all my doctor's bills, and now you're offering unlimited hospitality. So, what's the catch? What kind of price am I going to be expected to pay for all this generosity?' She could see his mouth beginning to set into an angry line, but that didn't intimidate her.

'What makes you think there's a price to be paid?' he said grimly.

'You're a very successful businessman, aren't you?' she challenged him.

'I run my company competently and efficiently,' he agreed. 'What the hell's that got to do with any of this?'

'A man doesn't get into your sort of position by giving anything away for free. That's how you *got* to the top, isn't it? By knowing the exact value of everything—including people!'

'Because I run my company to maximum efficiency, that doesn't automatically make me a complete bastard where my private life is concerned,' Lewis growled, his face glowering now.

'So now I'm part of your private life? And how did *that* happen?' demanded Lorel.

But Lewis had apparently run completely out patience. He muttered something under his breath; then he turned and strode towards the door.

'I'll wait for you in reception. And don't be long!' he instructed. 'Now that I've got my briefcase back, I need to make several extremely important phone calls.'

After he had gone, Lorel stood in the middle of the room for a couple of minutes, quietly fuming. He really was an exasperating and overbearing man! And why wouldn't he tell her what she wanted to know? She was absolutely certain by now that he was keeping a lot back from her. Why would he do that, though, unless he had something to hide? And what *was* it? She frowned irritably. Unless she remembered it for herself, it looked as if she was never going to find out.

She glanced round the room, and then frowned again. She had an even more pressing problem at the moment—what was she going to do now?

Common sense told her that she didn't actually have much choice. She was short of money—and short of friends. It looked as if she was going to have to take up Lewis's offer of hospitality at the Palazzo Gregolino. She needn't stay for long, she comforted herself. It shouldn't take more than a day or two to sort out her return ticket; then she could go back home.

She had to admit that she wasn't exactly thrilled by the thought of going back to England. There would be all the hassle of getting a new job, and trying to make a life for herself that was more interesting and fun than the last couple of years had been. It was going to take an enormous amount of effort on her part, and she wasn't sure that she had the energy or enthusiasm for it right now. Life in general seemed to have been one big muddle for such a long time, and no matter what she did, or how hard she tried, things only seemed to get worse, never better. Look at this holiday. She had planned to have a luxurious trip on the Orient-Express, and then spend a few fun days in Venice, hopefully meeting up with people of her own age and making new friends. Instead, she had somehow landed in a complete mess. She couldn't even *remember* her trip on the Orient-Express, and the only friend she had made was Lewis. Her mouth set into a wry grimace. Did he count as a friend? She really wasn't sure what category she ought to put him in!

One thing was pretty clear, though. He was the only person around right now who was offering any kind of help. Did that mean she was going to have to take him up on it? With a small sigh, she admitted there really didn't seem to be any alternative.

Reluctantly, she shoved her things into a suitcase. She took one last look around the room, to make sure she hadn't left anything behind, and then staggered downstairs with her luggage.

When they arrived back at the *palazzo*, Lewis immediately disappeared into the library, presumably to make his phone calls. Lorel went upstairs to unpack, and then she carefully put all the clothes Lewis had bought her into a neat pile, ready to return them to him.

She decided she might as well give them back to him right away. If he was still tied up with his phone calls, then she could just leave them somewhere he could easily find them.

As she reached the foot of the stairs, though, Lewis came out of the library. He glanced at her, and then his gaze shifted to the clothes she was carrying.

'What were you planning to do with those?' he enquired.

'I was going to give them back to you, of course.'

'And what am I meant to do with them?'

'I've no idea,' Lorel replied. 'Perhaps you could send them back to the boutique?'

'They've been worn, which makes them second-hand,' he pointed out. 'The boutique won't take them back again.'

'Well, I can't keep them,' she declared.

'Why not?'

'Because I can't afford them!'

Lewis's mouth shifted into a distinctly impatient line. 'No one's asked you to pay for them.'

'I'm certainly not accepting them as a gift,' Lorel shot back immediately.

'Because they came from me?'

'Of course not. I wouldn't take them from anyone.'

'You can carry independence a little too far,' he told her. 'They're a couple of skirts and dresses, that's all.'

'*Expensive* skirts and dresses,' she reminded him.

His eyes narrowed. 'That really does bother you, doesn't it? Why this big hang-up about money?'

Lorel's brows drew together darkly. 'I haven't got any hang-ups. I just like to earn what I spend, that's all. And I don't like taking gifts from people I don't even know very well.'

Lewis's gaze altered perceptibly. 'You don't think we know each other?' he challenged softly.

She could feel that nervous tingling running along her spine again. With an effort, she shook it off.

'I don't want to argue about this,' she said briskly. 'Now that I've got my own clothes back, I don't need these any more. What you do with them is entirely your business. I'm very grateful for the use of them, but I don't want to keep them.'

To her surprise, Lewis didn't argue with her any further. Instead, he took the clothes from her, tossed them on to a nearby chair, and then stood looking at her thoughtfully for a few moments.

'Well?' she demanded slightly belligerently, more unnerved than she cared to admit by that steady scrutiny. 'Is there something else you want to say to me?'

'Yes, there is. But not here, in the middle of the hall. Come into the drawing-room.'

She followed him into the room, with its massive pictures, decorative ceiling, ornate chandeliers, beautifully carved furniture, and handsome mosaic floor. It was a rather overwhelming room, with its richness of colour and the magnificence of its furnishings, but it certainly didn't overshadow the man who had just entered it. Lorel had the feeling that Lewis Elliott would stand out in any surroundings, no matter how splendid.

'All right,' she said with a touch of edginess. 'What do you want to say?'

'I thought you ought to know that I'm leaving for Florence first thing in the morning. I'll probably be there for several days.'

'Oh,' she said, in a rather deflated tone. She hadn't been expecting to hear something like that. 'Oh—I see. That changes the situation quite a lot, doesn't it? I suppose you want me to leave.'

'Did I say that?'

'Well—no. But I can hardly stay here after you've gone.'

'I don't see why not. If you're nervous about staying at the *palazzo* on your own, I'll arrange for Maria to sleep here overnight.'

'It's not that. I just thought——'

Amusement showed briefly in his eyes. 'Thought what? That I wouldn't trust you? That, since you stole my briefcase, I was afraid you might run off with a couple of paintings, or perhaps some of the rather nice silver that's lying around?'

'I'd never do anything like that!' she said hotly. 'You know that!' Then she flushed slightly. He didn't know any such thing. In his eyes, she had already proved herself a thief. She didn't have the slightest idea why she had taken his briefcase, but one fact stood out like a sore thumb. She definitely *had* taken it, so there was no reason why he shouldn't think her capable of stealing something else.

'I wouldn't take anything,' she muttered again, although without much hope that he would believe her.

'I didn't think for one moment that you would,' Lewis replied, to her complete astonishment. 'Let's drop the subject, and get back to my original question. Do you want to stay here, or not?'

'I don't know,' she said uncertainly.

'I thought it would be a good chance for you to see something of Venice. Your holiday was more or less ruined by that knock you took on your head. This would be an opportunity to make up for it.'

It certainly was a very tempting offer. 'How long could I stay?' she asked slowly.

'How about until I get back?'

Lorel raised her head. She hadn't realised he would be returning here, to the *palazzo*. She had assumed he would fly straight back to England from Florence.

'I'm not sure I get this,' she said slowly. 'Are you telling me that you want to see me again?'

One of Lewis's dark eyebrows lifted noticeably. 'Is that so incredible?'

'I just didn't expect it,' she said, rather defensively.

'Didn't you?' His soft challenge raised a whole load of new possibilities that she wasn't sure she wanted to explore just yet.

'You've already branded me a thief,' she reminded him, a sudden wave of nervousness making her tone sharp. 'And most of the time, I feel as if I've been nothing but a nuisance to you ever since you first clapped eyes on me. Now, you're suddenly offering me the use of this *palazzo*, and telling me you want me to stay here until you get back.'

Lewis's expression revealed absolutely nothing. 'Perhaps I just like girls with big brown eyes,' he suggested.

'That's silly!'

'Mmm. Maybe,' he murmured. 'Or do you think the romance of this city is beginning to get to me?'

Lorel's mouth twitched nervously. 'I don't think you've got a romantic bone in your body! And I don't know why you're winding me up like this.'

His blue eyes flickered for an instant, and then became still again. 'I think if anyone's getting wound up, then it's me.' He came a step nearer, and Lorel's stomach abruptly turned over. 'You *get* to me,' he went on, and his tone was a little thicker now. 'And I think you know exactly how much.'

She swallowed hard. 'I don't,' she whispered. 'I really don't.'

'Want me to show you?'

She didn't think that she did, but she couldn't seem to actually say so. Lewis took another couple of steps forward, and she gave an involuntary shiver as his shadow fell over her.

'Cold?' he said, noticing it. 'Or are you scared of me?' Then he shook his head. 'No, I don't think it's either of those things. Which leaves a much more interesting possibility...'

He was touching her before he had even finished speaking. One of his hands ran leisurely up her bare arm, and she shivered all over again, more convulsively this time.

'I'm shivering, too,' Lewis told her softly. 'Only inside, where you can't see it. Want to feel?' he invited.

He took her hand and slid it inside his jacket. As he pressed it flat against his lower chest, she could feel the tiny tremors racing over his skin.

'I don't know why you do this to me,' he went on huskily. 'But I like it. I definitely like it.'

'Well, I'm not at all sure that I do,' she flashed back at him. 'It's—it's——'

'A little frightening?' he suggested.

'You're always finishing my sentences for me,' Lorel muttered in annoyance.

'Perhaps that's because you always seem to end up a little speechless when I'm around. Or maybe you don't really want to talk at all,' he added, his gaze sliding over assessingly. 'Come to think of it, *I'm* rather tired of words...'

There was a whole lot more that Lorel wanted to say to him, though. It was just that she never got the chance. His mouth moved smoothly over hers before she got out a single syllable, and once the kiss got under way all thoughts of talking flew straight out of her head.

Lewis paused only to take a quick breath and mutter something appreciatively. Then the kiss began all over again, more fierce this time, as if he were tired of waiting for something he wanted so much.

His hands curled round her, inched their way down her spine, curved round the firm swell of her buttocks, and then relentlessly pulled her closer. His mouth didn't ease up for an instant, and the closeness of his body made her startlingly aware that he wanted very much more than just this kiss.

An indignant cough from the doorway made sure that he wasn't going to get it, though. Reluctantly but swiftly, he let go of her; then he turned to shoot an apologetic smile at Maria, who was standing there with her arms folded, glaring at him.

While Lewis launched into a smooth flow of Italian, obviously offering Maria some kind of explanation, Lorel slowly got her senses back. She still felt hot and flustered, though, and she had the feeling that they might very well have ended up on the comfortable sofa just behind them if Maria hadn't come in at that moment. To her alarm, she found that the idea didn't completely shock her.

After Maria had been placated, and gently but firmly shooed out of the room, Lorel stared at Lewis.

'What did you tell her?' she demanded.

'That I'm leaving for Florence in the morning, and that was just a friendly goodbye kiss.'

Lorel's eyebrows shot up. 'And she *believed* you?'

'Of course not,' replied Lewis cheerfully. 'And we won't get a chance to repeat it,' he added regretfully. 'Maria's going to spend the next few hours watching the two of us like a hawk. It looks as if she's personally taken on the task of safeguarding your virtue.'

Lorel wasn't sure if she was sorry about that, or not.

'What time are you leaving in the morning?' she asked.

'Early. I've got my first meeting scheduled for the afternoon. After that, it'll be more or less all work for the next few days.' His eyes gleamed regretfully. 'I wish I could take you with me.'

Lorel blinked. 'To Florence?'

'Yes. Unfortunately, it's just not possible. I'll be staying with some friends, and they're an extremely conservative Italian family. They'd be shocked—and insulted—if I turned up with an unattached and un-chaperoned female in tow.'

'I don't know that I even want to go to Florence,' she told him, with a rather poor attempt at defiance.

Lewis took absolutely no notice of her prickly tone. 'You'd like it. In its own way, it's just as beautiful as Venice.' His blue gaze fixed on her. 'Perhaps we could go at some other time?'

'You seem to be making a lot of plans without even consulting me,' Lorel said, a little resentfully. Over the last couple of years, she had got used to running her own life. She wasn't sure that she liked someone stepping in like this, and trying to take it over.

'I'm not trying to force you into anything,' Lewis pointed out. 'Just suggesting one or two things that might turn out to be fun.'

She gazed at him warily. 'Your idea of fun is probably very different from mine.'

'It's possible,' he agreed. Then his mouth curled lazily into a smile. 'But think how nice it would be if it turned out to be exactly the same.' His eyes locked on to hers, and steadily held her gaze. 'Do you suppose there's any chance of that, Lorel?' he questioned her softly.

'I shouldn't think so,' she forced herself to say, but somehow there wasn't the slightest hint of conviction in her voice.

Lewis's eyes never left hers for an instant. She began to feel as if she were drowning in his vivid blue gaze.

'And do you think you'll still be here when I return from Florence?' he challenged her.

Lorel tried to remember that she was fully inde-pendent. She didn't have to let any man—and cer-tainly not this man—make her decisions for her. If only his eyes weren't so damned hypnotic! She could almost feel her will-power floating away on a tide of deep blue...

'*Will* you be here?' Lewis repeated.

'I don't know—I might be—probably will be——' she admitted weakly, furious with herself for sounding so completely feeble, but quite incapable of doing anything about it.

Lewis looked as if he had never been in any real doubt about it. 'Then I'll see you when I get back. Once I've tied up my business affairs in Florence, we'll have all the time we need to sort out where we go from here.'

Lorel wasn't at all sure that she wanted to go anywhere, not with Lewis Elliott. She seemed to have run clean out of arguments for the moment, though. In fact, even standing up straight was annoyingly difficult. There was a definite sensation of weakness around her knees.

You'll feel a lot better once he's gone, she tried to convince herself. He makes you nervous, hanging around, kissing you when you're not expecting it, and dropping all those odd hints about the future.

She bit her lip nervously, and knew that she was going to wait for his return with a mixture of apprehension and excitement.

CHAPTER EIGHT

ALTHOUGH Lorel was up early the next morning, she found Lewis had already left. She tried to convince herself that she was relieved. She also tried to convince herself—although with an equal lack of success—that she still had a choice. She could leave any time she liked. She certainly didn't have to hang around here until Lewis returned, not if she didn't want to.

Then Lorel sighed. What was the point in trying to kid herself? She *did* want to stay. She didn't have the slightest idea what Lewis was doing to her, but she did know it would take a major catastrophe to shift her out of the Palazzo Gregolino before he returned.

With Lewis gone, the days seemed unexpectedly long. Although Lorel filled them with a concentrated programme of sightseeing, the hours still dragged. And Venice itself seemed to have lost a lot of its magical glitter now that she wasn't sharing it with Lewis. She dutifully trudged around churches and museums, she rode up and down the canals in *vaporetti*, admired paintings, gazed at statues, and fed the pigeons in St Mark's Square. She took a trip out to Murano, to visit the glass-making factories, explored the Doge's Palace, and pottered round the markets. And all the while she was aware that she was just filling in time. What she was really doing was waiting for Lewis to return.

She was rather alarmed by this discovery of her intense interest in him. It seemed to have crept up on her and caught her unawares, and now she couldn't shake it off. She wasn't even sure that she wanted to, and that alarmed her even more.

'You don't know anything about him,' she told herself more than once. Then she would sigh. That wasn't strictly true. There were all the things he had already told her, and a whole lot more which he hadn't actually put into words, but which she could guess at. For instance, the fact that he led an unexpectedly lonely life. He couldn't relate to his stepmother or stepbrother, and though he was clearly very fond of his stepsister, she had now married and moved away from him. His business life seemed to leave him with little time for personal relationships, and she had the feeling that he was a man who wasn't particularly interested in casual affairs.

Lorel furrowed her brow. There were still huge gaps in her knowledge of him; she was well aware of that. Yet something was telling her that it wouldn't be too difficult to close those gaps—if she wanted to.

By the end of the week, she seemed to have a permanent headache. She told herself it was from tension, and tried to relax. For a while, she felt a bit better. Then she woke up the next morning feeling distinctly nauseous, and with a small groan, crawled back under the covers and lay there feeling very sorry for herself.

'Too much of Maria's cooking,' she muttered weakly, and was sure that was the cause of her queasy stomach. Maria kept piling up her plate with enough food for half a dozen people, and Lorel always valiantly tackled it, not wanting to offend her by leaving any.

When Maria came in later and found her still in bed, she fussed around endlessly, which made Lorel feel even worse. The Italian woman was obviously agitated that Lorel had become ill while Lewis was away. In the end, Lorel forced herself out of bed just to try and put Maria's mind at rest.

In fact, she felt rather better once she was up. By tea time, she could even face a light meal—which fortunately turned out to be salad, with no sign of the pasta which had been turning up in such huge quantities all week.

Next morning, she was up fairly early and tottering around, although she couldn't honestly say she felt much better. The queasiness was back again, along with an unpleasant dizziness which only gradually eased off as the day wore on. She abandoned the sightseeing programme she had worked out for the day. There was no way she could face a tiring tramp around the streets of Venice feeling like this.

She spent the next couple of days flopped out lethargically in a chair most of the time, either dozing or rather half-heartedly skimming through a paperback. When there was enough warmth in the sun, she moved out into the small, walled garden at the back of the *palazzo*. Worn stone statues peered out from behind overgrown bushes, grass and weeds pushed their way up in between the flagstones, and the entire garden could obviously do with the attention of a keen gardener, but Lorel liked it just the way it was. The quiet peacefulness and the fresh air made her feel much better.

It was nearly a week and a half now since Lewis had left. During that time, she had heard from him only a handful of times. His last call had come a couple of days ago, to say that his business in Florence was taking rather longer than he had expected. He hadn't spoken to her for long—there had been voices in the background, and she assumed he was at some sort of meeting or reception—but he had promised to be back at the *palazzo* before the following weekend.

In fact, he returned on Thursday evening. Lorel was dozing on the sofa in the drawing-room, and didn't actually hear him come in. What woke her up was the sound of Maria's voice, launching into a dramatic flood of Italian. Blinking sleepily, Lorel then heard Lewis's voice asking a couple of sharp questions. Maria answered volubly, her voice rising and falling with emotion, and Lorel groaned. She could guess what Maria was telling Lewis. Her minor illness was being given the full soap opera treatment! Lewis was going to walk in expecting to find her wan and wasted, almost too weak to twitch her little finger.

She hauled herself off the sofa, and had just got to her feet when Lewis strode into the room. For just a moment, the sight of him sent a weakness flooding through her that had absolutely nothing to do with her queasy stomach or dizzy head. Then the room slowly steadied again, her legs felt just about able to hold her up, and she managed a pleased, if feeble, smile.

'Hello, Lewis.'

'What the hell's been going on?' he growled. 'Maria's just spun me some tale about you being too ill to get out of bed.' His blue gaze raked over her. 'You look fine to me.'

'I *am* fine,' she said, with a touch of exasperation. 'Well, that's not quite true,' she conceded. 'I've had some kind of virus, and been rather off-colour. I'm much better now, though.'

Lewis didn't look convinced. 'What sort of symptoms have you had?' he asked curtly.

She shrugged. 'Nothing too exciting. I've felt a bit sick, and rather tired. And now and then, I get a bit dizzy.' She wrinkled her nose. 'Can't we talk about something more interesting than my ailments?'

'Not when you've so recently had a bad knock on the head,' Lewis replied. 'You could be suffering from delayed concussion. I'll get the doctor round first thing in the morning, to take a look at you.'

'I don't need a doctor!' she insisted. 'I'm all right.'

'Perhaps you are, but I don't intend to take any chances. Get yourself off to bed, and Maria will bring you up some hot milk.'

'Lewis, it's only eight o'clock! I'm not ten years old, I can stay up to whatever time I like. And I *hate* hot milk,' she added grumpily.

'If the doctor says you're OK after he's looked at you, then you can stay up all night drinking whatever you like. Until then, you'll behave sensibly. Bed!' he ordered.

'But you've only just got back,' Lorel protested. She gave him her most wistful smile. 'We haven't even had a chance to talk.'

The smile didn't work. 'Upstairs,' said Lewis implacably. 'And right now!'

She fluttered her eyelashes at him innocently. 'Are you going to come with me? To make sure I don't get a sudden dizzy spell, and fall down the stairs?'

His blue eyes darkened several shades. 'Don't tempt me,' he warned. 'I've had an exhausting couple of weeks, and a long journey. There's nothing I'd like better than to find some way of relaxing—and I can think of several things I'd find *very* relaxing,' he added in a tone that set her nerves gently quivering.

Lorel hastily decided that it was time for the teasing to stop. 'Er—perhaps you're right, I'd better get some rest. Goodnight.' She moved towards the door, then paused for a moment. 'I'm glad you're back, Lewis,' she said in a quieter voice. Then she turned round and ran lightly up the stairs.

She slept well that night, but woke up in the morning feeling distinctly off colour again.

'Oh, damn!' she muttered impatiently. The room wavered about uncomfortably as soon as she lifted her head from the pillow, and her stomach felt distinctly rocky.

Maria brought her breakfast on a tray, but she couldn't manage more than a few mouthfuls of fresh fruit juice. When Lewis came in half an hour later, a light frown shadowed his face.

'Maria said you couldn't eat anything this morning.'

'It was probably Maria's cooking that caused this problem in the first place,' Lorel said rather crossly. 'She's absolutely stuffed me with food all the time you've been away. I feel as if I've been force-fed!'

A gleam of a smile replaced the frown on Lewis's dark features. 'Italian men tend to like their women well-proportioned. She probably thinks you stand a better chance of finding a husband if you put on a few more pounds.'

Lorel glared at him. 'Are you saying I'm too thin?'

'Compared to Maria, you're positively anorexic. But I don't think there's very much about you that I'd actually want to change.'

'How very magnanimous of you!' She squirmed a little further down into the bed. 'So, what am I supposed to do now? Stay here until I've been prodded and poked by the doctor?'

'Yes,' came Lewis's calm reply. 'Then we'll see if he'll allow you to get up or not.'

She scowled. 'I hate being molly-coddled.'

'Then do whatever the doctor instructs. That way, you'll soon be on your feet again.'

Lorel's own eyes suddenly glittered with pure mischief. Then she batted her eyelashes at him. 'Are you sure that's where you want me?' she purred. 'On my *feet*?'

Lewis shot a warning glance at her. 'If you don't want the doctor to walk in and find us both in a very compromising position, you'd better cut that out!' He turned towards the door. 'I'll come back later, with the doctor.'

'Safety in numbers?' she taunted him, with a grin.

Lewis growled something under his breath. Then, with obvious reluctance, he left the room.

After he had gone, Lorel fluffed up the pillows, trying to make them more comfortable. She was already beginning to feel brighter. The dizziness had gone, and she was actually beginning to feel hungry. She hoped the doctor wouldn't be late. She didn't want to spend half the day stuck in bed.

He arrived promptly at ten o'clock. It was the same doctor who had treated her after her fall, and he smiled at her as he came into the room. Then he murmured something comforting in Italian. She had to admit he had a very good bedside manner.

As before, all his questions to her had to be put through Lewis, who then translated her answers back

to the doctor. He examined her head, and seemed satisfied with what he found. Then, through Lewis, she
had to describe her symptoms to him. The doctor
listened carefully, sat back and thought about it for
a short while, and then began to ask her some more
questions.

Some of them were a lot more personal than she
had expected, and she flushed slightly as she gave the
answers. What did he want to know all those details
for? Then there was another pause while the doctor
seemed to consider what she had told him. Finally,
he turned and quietly asked Lewis something.

Lorel had no idea what his question had been—her
Italian was still at the totally basic stage—but Lewis's
reaction was certainly pretty disconcerting. His face
changed abruptly, he clearly paled under his light tan,
and then he snapped back with a couple of questions
of his own.

The doctor looked rather surprised, as if this wasn't
the reaction he had expected from Lewis. Then he
spoke again at some length.

Lewis's face had gone so grim now that Lorel
became quite alarmed. What on earth had the doctor
said? Was there something awful wrong with her?

'What's going on?' she asked, a note of panic in
her voice. 'Lewis, what does the doctor think is wrong
with me?'

Lewis didn't answer, but the doctor must have
caught the note of fear in her voice, because he turned
and smiled at her reassuringly. Then he spoke to her
cheerfully, and although she didn't have the slightest
idea what he was saying Lorel immediately felt better.
There couldn't be anything too wrong, or he would
be looking a lot more sombre.

The doctor picked up his bag, said something else to Lewis, who was still glowering fiercely, and then smiled again at Lorel as he said goodbye to her.

After he had left the room, Lorel turned to Lewis with a small frown. 'What was that all about? And why did he keep calling me *"signora"*?' she added. 'Surely he knows I'm not married?'

'Since the two of us are living under the same roof, he automatically assumed——' Lewis broke off rather abruptly, and seemed oddly tense.

Lorel suddenly saw the light, and a broad grin spread over her face. 'Oh, I get it. He thought I was married to *you*. No wonder you looked rather po-faced just now! But why didn't you just explain the situation to him?'

'That didn't seem like a very good idea,' muttered Lewis darkly.

'Why not? Oh, I know he'd have been shocked,' she went on. 'But you could have explained that we're not actually *living* together. I'm sure he'd have understood.'

'Lorel, will you just shut up?' he ordered tersely.

Suspicion began to spread through her again. 'There's something wrong, isn't there?' she said slowly. 'You're acting really weird.' Her brows drew together in a worried frown. 'That doctor told you something about me—and I want to know what it was!'

'I don't think that you do,' he replied grimly. He turned away from her and prowled over to the window.

Panic started to flutter in her stomach again. 'Is it bad?'

'Bad?' He gave a brief, humourless laugh. 'That rather depends on your point of view. But it's sure as hell going to come as a shock.'

Lorel's throat had gone uncomfortably dry. 'What kind of a shock?'

'The type that knocks you completely off your feet,' Lewis replied, swinging round to face her again.

She sat up very straight in the bed. 'All right,' she said steadily. 'You'd better tell me what it is.'

Lewis looked as if he would prefer to be anywhere except here, in this bedroom, face to face with her. 'The doctor could be wrong,' he said at last. 'He admitted that himself. It's just a shrewd guess, based on what you told him, and his own observations.'

'Lewis, will you stop beating round the bush and just come out with it?' she snapped angrily. 'What did he say?'

His blue gaze fixed on her with even deeper intensity. 'He thought it highly likely that you're in the very early stages of pregnancy.'

Lorel released a huge sigh of relief. 'And I thought you were going to come out with something really serious! Honestly, Lewis, what did you wind me up like that for? I thought I was practically on my deathbed!'

His eyes narrowed. 'I didn't think you'd take it like this.'

'Why on earth not?' she said brightly. 'I've got a sense of humour, haven't I? I mean, it's easy to see how he made such a mistake. He assumed we were married—and like an idiot, you didn't tell him we weren't—and my system *has* been a bit upset since that knock on the head.' Lorel grinned. 'No wonder you went such an odd colour when he came out with that diagnosis! I suppose it's really rather funny, when you think about it.'

'Can you see me laughing?' Lewis asked a little tautly.

'Well—no. But it's not my fault if you don't laugh a lot. You really ought to try and be less strait-laced.'

'I did try that once,' Lewis informed her softly. 'On the Orient-Express, when I met a girl who somehow got to me in a way that was quite new to me.'

Lorel stopped grinning. 'I don't remember any of that,' she reminded him, with a sudden fluttering of unease.

'I know you don't. But I do—very clearly.' He came a little closer to the bed. 'When the hell *are* you going to remember it, Lorel?'

'Would it make any difference if I did?'

'Oh, yes,' he told her in a very even voice. 'Because then you'd know that the doctor's diagnosis might not be as way-out as you seem to think it is.'

Lorel was suddenly very glad that she was still in bed, because a huge wave of weakness had just swept over her.

'Exactly what are you saying?' she somehow managed to get out.

His eyes flickered with sudden impatience. 'You want me to put it bluntly? We slept together,' Lewis told her crudely. 'Which means there's every chance that the doctor's right, and you *are* pregnant. So— how do you feel about becoming a parent, Lorel Parker?'

She stared at him with stunned shock. 'I don't believe any of this!' she said shakily at last, although it was suddenly a fairly weak sort of protest. His words had a horrible ring of truth about them. Anyway, why would he be making any of this up?

'Believe it!' Lewis ordered tensely. 'Better still, dig past that barrier you've put up inside your mind, and remember it for yourself.'

But she didn't want to do that. She didn't even want to listen to any more of this.

She turned her head away from him. 'I think you'd better get out of here,' she told him tautly.

Lewis didn't budge an inch. 'I'm not going anywhere. There's too much we need to discuss.'

At that, she lifted her head and flung a hot glance at him. 'There is nothing to discuss! I don't know why you're doing this to me, but I'm not going to let you go on with it any longer. I know what I would and wouldn't do. And I'd never—*never* sleep with someone I'd only just met.'

'Just as you'd never steal anything that didn't belong to you? Such as a briefcase?' he shot back at her. 'But you did steal it,' Lewis reminded her, in a harsh tone. 'And you did sleep with me.' His eyes briefly glittered. 'It isn't the sort of thing I'm ever likely to forget.'

Lorel glared at him. 'Well, if it really happened, then it couldn't have been too good for me, because I couldn't wait to forget it! And if it *did* happen, then there's only one possible explanation for it. You forced me into it!'

Lewis's gaze blazed so brightly that she instinctively flinched back from him.

'I have never forced a woman in my life,' he grated.

But Lorel clung to that explanation as if it were a vital lifeline. 'You must have done,' she insisted, with total conviction. Further light dawned inside her head.

'And that's why I stole your briefcase, isn't it? Because I wanted to get back at you in any way I could!'

Lewis growled irritably under his breath. 'It's pointless arguing with you right now. This must have come as quite a shock. You need time to get used to the idea, and adjust to the situation.'

Something inside her head suddenly snapped. 'I don't need to adjust. I already know what the truth is!' she yelled at him. 'And no one is going to make me change my mind about it.'

He swung round and strode over to the door. 'We'll talk about this later. And don't try to leave,' he warned darkly. 'You're not setting foot outside the *palazzo* until we've made some definite decisions about the future.'

After he had gone, Lorel slumped back on to the pillows, all the defiance draining straight out of her as soon as Lewis was out of sight. This was the very last thing on earth she had been expecting. Her mind started to whirl round and round in circles. How could she possibly have slept with Lewis, and not remember it? But the only other explanation was that he was lying, and what motive could he have for that? Anyway, she had the horrible feeling that he was telling the truth. She remembered the shocked look on Lewis's face when the doctor had given his diagnosis—he certainly hadn't been feigning that!

But—pregnant! She gave a small moan. She certainly didn't *feel* pregnant. Her hands began to move gingerly over her body, trying to spot any changes. She couldn't find any, but she supposed it was too early for any to show. She gave another groan. There must be some kind of test she could take, to find out for certain one way or the other.

On the other hand, it might be even worse knowing for sure. Then she would have to accept that the impossible had happened, and she had actually slept with Lewis Elliott.

Lorel turned on to her stomach and buried her face in the pillow. She wanted to go to sleep, and then wake up again to find this had all been a freakish nightmare. A few minutes later, though, she hauled herself out of bed and pulled on a dressing-gown. She wasn't going to be able to wish herself out of this situation. All she could do was somehow face up to it, and try to get a few basic facts sorted out.

She quickly showered and dressed. When she was finally ready to go downstairs, she stopped for a moment and studied her reflection in the mirror. She was surprised to find that she didn't look any different from usual. A little pale, perhaps, but she always went rather wan when she was feeling off colour. Her gold-brown hair hadn't lost its gloss and bounce, though, her eyes looked bright and alert, and her mouth looked innocently demure.

Well, according to Lewis, she certainly *wasn't* an innocent, she reminded herself shakily. Then, with reluctance, she left the bedroom and went down the stairs.

Lewis was in the drawing-room. The tall doors that led on to the terrace and garden at the back of the *palazzo* were standing wide open, as if he felt in need of fresh air. The sun patterned the ground with golden reflections and dappled shadows, but Lorel was in no mood to appreciate the peaceful scene.

'I want to know exactly what happened,' she told Lewis bluntly, as soon as she had walked into the room.

Lewis turned round slowly. His dark brows were drawn together, and he looked as if he had a pounding headache, but she didn't particularly care about that.

'I've already told you,' he said evenly.

'Not the details!'

His mouth compressed itself into an even tighter line. 'I thought you didn't want to go into them, since you obviously find the whole thing so distasteful.'

'No one likes the idea of being forced into something,' she retorted.

Lewis took a couple of quick steps towards her, but then made a clear effort to stop himself. 'You weren't forced!' he said sharply.

She flung a look of open disbelief back at him. 'Then how did it happen?'

This time, his blue eyes didn't falter. 'If you like, I'll show you exactly how it happened,' he offered softly.

Lorel instantly shook her head. She wasn't going to let him sidetrack her in any way. She knew all too well how susceptible she was to this man's touch and kisses. Once he got his hands on her, he might be able to persuade her to believe all sorts of things.

She blinked nervously. Was that how it had been on the train? Had she already been highly vulnerable to Lewis Elliott's influence? If she had been, then everything might have happened just the way he had said. She might have given in to him quite willingly...

Then she firmly straightened her shoulders. She wouldn't—couldn't—believe that. If she ever did, her entire world would start to crumble.

'Let's get down to practical matters,' she said in a hard voice. 'The doctor wasn't certain I was pregnant. He could well be wrong. Probably *is* wrong,' she added with emphasis, as if there were little doubt in her own mind.

'He seemed to think there was a good chance he was right,' Lewis replied.

'I want to know for certain. I want a proper test—and soon!'

'I'll arrange it. What if it proves positive?' Lewis questioned her tautly.

'I'm sure it won't.' She hoped she sounded a lot more confident than she felt.

'But if it does?'

'Then there are still all sorts of options,' she said steadily. 'It's very early. An abortion would be easy——'

'You wouldn't do that,' Lewis interrupted her.

His arrogant assumption infuriated her. 'Just try me!' she snarled back at him. 'This is my body. Don't you ever try to tell me what I can or can't do with it!'

Lewis shook his head. 'I don't even have to argue with you about it. I know what you can or can't do, and still live easily with yourself.'

Lorel glared at him furiously. 'You do *not* know me.'

'Oh, but I do,' he assured her softly. 'And a whole lot better than you even realise. So, let's drop all these pointless threats of abortion, and consider the alternatives.'

The infuriating thing, of course, was that he was right. Although she was angry enough to fling the threat of an abortion in his face, she knew perfectly well that she would back away from it when the time came. Something inside her just wouldn't let her go ahead with it.

'What sort of alternatives did you have in mind?' she muttered at last, in a dark tone.

'There's one rather obvious, although hackneyed one,' came his calm reply. 'Marriage.'

'Marriage?' she yelped. 'Are you mad?'

'Not certifiably so. Although there are definitely times when you drive me more than a little crazy!'

'I am not marrying you,' she stated with utter determination.

'I haven't actually asked you yet,' he pointed out. 'I was just putting it up as a possible solution to the situation.'

'Forget it,' she advised him. 'If you can't come up with anything better than that, then just go away. Leave me to cope with this on my own.'

'I told you once before, I've got a certain sense of responsibility. I don't walk away from my commitments.'

Lorel's face grew even more stormy. 'I am not a "commitment". Don't go lumping me together with your stepmother and stepbrother, just another great millstone hanging round your neck!'

His eyes gleamed for an instant. 'That isn't quite the way I see you.'

'Well, it certainly sounded like it to me.'

'Then I apologise,' Lewis said, to her total astonishment. 'But I do think you ought to consider the possibility of marriage. Look at it from a purely practical point of view. You don't have any family, any job, or anyone you can turn to. Marriage to me would solve all those problems.'

'When I get married, it won't be for any practical reasons!' Lorel howled back at him in outrage. 'I want to *love* my husband.'

'And you don't think you could love me?' Lewis asked, just a little too casually.

'You're the most unlovable man I've ever met!' She was still so angry that the lie slipped easily off her tongue.

'Think about it,' he advised. 'You could do a lot worse.'

'Oh, sure,' she retorted. 'I could marry a gorilla! They've got a certain rough charm, as well.'

Lewis drew in an impatient breath. 'There's no point in going on with this conversation while you're in this mood. We'd better leave it until you've calmed down.'

'Calmed down!' Lorel exploded. 'And how long do you think that's going to take? Ten minutes? Half an hour? Then I'll be able to look at this whole thing rationally? Let me tell you something,' she went on in a voice that had begun to shake with pure emotion, 'you can wait until hell freezes over, and I still won't have got over this! You tell me I've slept with you, and yet I can't remember a single second of it. In fact, you didn't just sleep with me, it looks as if you've made me pregnant—but to me, the whole thing's a total blank! Probably the most important moment in my life, and as far as I'm concerned, it didn't even happen! That's not the kind of thing you *ever* get over!'

It gave her a great deal of satisfaction to see the colour drain from Lewis's face. She thought he was going to say something more. Instead, though, to her surprise, he turned round and silently strode from the room, as if he had suddenly run completely out of words.

Once he had gone, she collapsed into a chair, shaking uncontrollably now. She felt as if she didn't want to see Lewis ever again. Then, with a fresh pang, she realised that wasn't a very practical proposition. If she was pregnant, then she could hardly go on avoiding the father of her child for the rest of her life.

Lewis left her alone until after lunch. To her astonishment, she found she was starving hungry, and she ate everything Maria set in front of her. Maria smiled at her approvingly, but Lorel couldn't smile back. Her appetite might have approved, but she was still clean out of smiles.

Lewis returned shortly afterwards. 'I've been giving some more thought to this question of marriage,' he informed her, as he sat down opposite her.

'Really?' questioned Lorel with freezing politeness. 'Do I know the unlucky woman you're planning to propose to?'

'Cut it out, Lorel,' he growled, 'I need to get this straightened out—and now.'

'That's probably because you're a businessman,' she replied coldly, somehow managing to stay amazingly in control of herself. 'You like to have everything cut and dried, and neatly filed away. Unfortunately, life's often a bit too messy to sort out that easily.'

Lewis managed to hold on to his temper.

'I don't see any reason why we *shouldn't* get married. We get on well——'

'Get on well?' she interrupted incredulously.

'Things were going fine between us before this happened,' he reminded her.

Lorel decided she didn't want to think about that. 'That's only because I didn't know the truth about you,' she retorted.

He ignored that remark. 'I think that, basically, we like each other——' he began again.

'And do you think that's enough to hold a marriage together?' Lorel interrupted rudely.

'No. But we've got a lot more going for us than just that. And we're not exactly strangers, Lorel.' The expression in his eyes told her a great deal more than his words.

'It seems to me that you know a whole lot more about me than I do about you,' Lorel said very pointedly.

Lewis's mouth curved into an unexpected smile. 'We could easily remedy that.'

Her eyebrows shot up. 'We certainly could not! One night in bed with you was apparently enough to make me lose my memory. I don't know what you did to me, but I certainly don't want to repeat it!'

His expression abruptly changed. 'I didn't hurt you, or make you do a single thing against your will.'

'That's *your* version of events.'

'Then make an effort to remember it for yourself!' Lewis threw back at her tersely. 'I don't know why you're so damned well determined to forget it. You enjoyed every single second of it . . .' His voice broke off, and a more thoughtful expression entered his eyes. 'Perhaps that's it,' he said more slowly. 'You don't want to forget it because you *hated* it, but because you liked it too much. It scared you, feeling that strongly about someone you hardly even knew. Perhaps you even felt guilty, if you're not used to a physical relationship with a man.'

'Oh, I've had enough of this!' she announced, getting to her feet and pushing the chair back forcefully. 'I'm going into the garden, for some fresh air.

And if you follow me out there, I think I'll probably scream—and very loudly!'

He didn't follow her, but when she finally came back into the *palazzo* he was waiting for her. The subject he wanted to discuss was the same one as before—marriage. Now that he had got the idea fixed into his head, he didn't seem to want to talk about anything else. At any other time, Lorel might have found his proposal flattering and rather exciting—even tempting, she had to admit. Right now, though, she was sick of hearing about it. Her head was spinning, she felt physically drained, and she had long since passed the point where she could think straight. The day had started off more or less like any other day, but had turned into a very bad dream that just wouldn't go away. She longed for some peace and quiet; some time to herself to try and get things straight inside her head; and, more than anything, to be somewhere there was *no Lewis Elliott*.

Half-way through the evening, she crawled up to bed, aching for sleep but absolutely certain it would be a long and restless night. She had just reached the bedroom door when Lewis materialised out of the dark shadows at the far end of the corridor.

'I thought I'd try one last proposal before you go to bed,' he told her. 'It struck me that this might be a good time to catch you in a mellow mood.'

Lorel couldn't even be bothered to argue with him any more. 'The answer is no,' she told him flatly.

When he next spoke, his voice was a little less casual. 'That sounded like a very definite decision.'

'I'm glad I'm finally getting through to you. Because it *is* definite,' she assured him grimly. 'And do you want to know why?'

Lewis suddenly looked rather tired and bleak. 'I thought we'd already been over all the reasons.'

'Well, let's go over the main one just once more, to make sure you've got it,' Lorel replied, without compunction. 'I won't even think about marriage to you until I know what happened on that train. For all I know, you *did* force me. You say you didn't, but I've only got your word for that. There's no way I'm going to risk getting tied up with a man who could do something like that.'

Lewis's expression changed, the bleakness sweeping away, to be replaced with a mixture of grimness and sudden determination.

'All right,' he said, catching hold of her arm. 'If those are your conditions, then we'd better get your memory back as soon as we can.'

Wariness made her eyes shoot wide open. 'How?'

'It's quite simple,' he told her, opening the bedroom door and then levering her inside. 'We'll repeat what happened that night, step by step, until we finally reach a point where you can't help but remember.' As her eyes opened even wider, he slid one hand down to her breast and fixed her with his fierce blue gaze. 'And I don't care how far I have to go,' he warned huskily. 'Before either of us leave this room again, you're going to know that you went willingly to bed with me that night!'

CHAPTER NINE

LOREL broke away from him quite easily. He had only been holding her very lightly.

'That's a totally crazy idea,' she told him shakily. 'And it won't work——'

'We won't know until we give it a try. And we *are* going to do that,' Lewis assured her softly.

Nervousness turned her legs to jelly. 'It'll only make things worse,' she insisted.

His gaze steadily held hers. 'How could things possibly get worse than they are right now?' He came nearer. 'Don't be a coward, Lorel. Or don't you want to remember?' came his direct challenge.

'Of course I do.' Then she bit her lip. Was that the strict truth? She wasn't sure any more. What if it turned out that Lewis had been telling the truth all along, and she really had jumped happily into bed with him? Her opinion of herself would slump to an all-time low, and she desperately didn't want that to happen. Her life had already been thrown completely off balance. She didn't want to end up despising herself, on top of that.

Lewis was advancing towards her again, though, and there was a very purposeful look in his eyes now. That, and a hot brightness which didn't scare her, as perhaps it should have, but instead sent a pleasant tingling sensation skittering over her skin.

'You were wearing a black velvet dress that night,' he told her. 'It felt soft to the touch—but not as soft as your skin.'

She remembered the dress. Remembered buying it; adding the gold embroidery that had made a splash of bright colour on one shoulder. She *didn't* remember wearing it.

'You've kissed me again since that night,' Lewis reminded her. 'You know there's nothing very alarming about a kiss.'

'I suppose not,' she muttered.

He shifted position again, leaving barely a couple of inches of space between them this time.

'Then perhaps we'll try just a kiss to start with,' he suggested smoothly.

Lorel wasn't convinced that was a very good idea, but she had the feeling that she wasn't going to be given any choice.

As it turned out, she was right. Lewis closed in on her easily but quickly, and his kiss was unexpectedly soft, but very thorough. It was nice—Lorel was willing to admit that—but all of his kisses had been nice. None of them had succeeded in jogging her memory, though, and this one wasn't accomplishing that, either.

She knew that Lewis had realised it, as well, but he wasn't giving up on the kiss. In fact, she had the impression that he was finding it increasingly hard to remember exactly why he was doing this. Other, more driving motives were beginning to take over, and she felt him finally resist them with a shudder.

'I didn't think this was going to be quite so difficult,' he murmured drily.

'Then perhaps you ought to give up on it right now,' Lorel said, with growing unease.

Lewis's eyes glittered. 'Once I've made up my mind to do something, I never give up on it,' he informed her.

Lorel had been afraid of that. She supposed she ought to protest more vehemently, make more of an effort to put a stop to this before it went too far, but she couldn't quite seem to manage it. She was suddenly very tired, and she just didn't have the energy. The day had lurched from crisis to crisis, and though she had coped with all of them after a fashion, she had run out of reserves now. Besides, Lewis's hands felt warm and soothing as they moved lightly over her. Just a while ago, she had been certain she never even wanted to see him again. Now, she was almost glad he was here. She was very aware of his male warmth and strength, and she desperately needed something like that right now; someone totally reliable she could lean on.

Did Lewis really fit that bill? asked a small, incredulous voice inside her head. Without him, you wouldn't be in this mess in the first place.

Lorel supposed there was a logical argument in there somewhere, but her muzzy head couldn't seem to figure out what it was. Anyway, instinct was taking over, and telling her to trust this man.

'Mad,' she muttered to herself.

Lewis raised his head for a moment. 'What?'

'Mad,' she repeated, her eyes drooping with weariness. 'That's what I am.'

'I don't think so.' He looked at her more closely. 'You're not going to fall asleep on me, are you?'

'Probably not.'

His fingers sidled inside her blouse, slid under the soft silk of her bra, and then gently pinched the already highly sensitive tip of her breast.

As Lorel's eyes flew wide open again, he smiled down at her. 'Just making sure you stay awake for a while longer.'

'Did I fall asleep on you on the train?'

'Not until quite a long while afterwards,' Lewis told her. His fingers kept moving thoughtfully while he spoke, sending small tremors right through Lorel's nervous system. 'You're not trying to stop me any more,' he observed quietly.

'Could I?'

'If you do it right now. Leave it for a few more minutes—and probably not,' came his husky admission.

She laid one hand against his chest, feeling the warmth of his body through the thin material of his shirt. 'Why do you make me feel like this?' she muttered in confusion. 'You get close to me, and I want——'

'Want what?' Lewis prompted.

'Want *you*,' she whispered reluctantly.

The front of her blouse was undone now, and he had released the catch on her bra, so that the full softness of her breast was available for him to tease and play with.

'Why do you suppose that is?' he questioned her a little thickly, his palm cupping the smooth swell in his palm.

'Don't know,' she mumbled.

'Don't know? Or just don't want to admit it?'

She looked up at him languidly. 'Don't want to admit it,' she conceded.

Lewis's hands provoked fresh shivers of pleasure. 'I could probably force a confession out of you,' he warned.

'I expect you could,' she agreed. A flicker of curiosity showed in her eyes. 'Are you really that interested?'

'Yes.'

She shrugged. 'Well, if you really want to know—it's because you *make* me want you. But I don't know how you do it.' A light frown crossed her face. 'That's not fair, is it? It means you're taking advantage of me. That makes you rather a bastard, Lewis Elliott.'

'Does it? Think about it a bit more, Lorel. Just what is it that gives me that advantage over you?'

Lorel wrinkled her nose. He was making her say things that she wanted to keep private, at least for a while longer. The words just seemed to be slipping out of her, though. She guessed it was because she was too tired to have much control over them any more.

'I suppose it's because I'm just a little bit in love with you,' she admitted with deep reluctance.

Lewis seemed to become unexpectedly tense for an instant. Then she felt his rigid muscles relax again, and when he next spoke it was in a very different tone of voice.

'Only a little bit?'

'Yes,' she said firmly. That was definitely all she was willing to tell him for now.

'Just one more thing. Are you ready to admit that I didn't force you into bed with me that night on the train?'

Lorel sighed. 'I suppose so,' she said grudgingly. 'I mean, considering everything that's happened, it doesn't seem very likely, does it?'

'Not very,' Lewis agreed. Then, to her surprise, he took a step back from her.

'What are you doing?' she asked.

'I think it's about time I went back to my own room.'

'But I thought——' She stopped rather abruptly, and a light flush of colour spread over her face.

'Yes, so did I,' agreed Lewis, with a touch of rue-fulness. 'But you're half-asleep on your feet.'

'I could stay awake for another five minutes,' Lorel told him in a low voice.

'The way I feel right now, five minutes is about all it would take!' Lewis commented drily.

'I don't think that would matter too much.'

She heard him draw in a quick breath. 'Don't tempt me,' he warned in a much rougher tone. 'I told you before, you get to me all too easily.'

'Why?' she asked softly.

But he looked as if he didn't want to answer that question. She knew perfectly well what he did want, though. There was no mistaking the heightened colour of his face, or the vivid brightness of his eyes.

'This won't solve anything,' he muttered. 'We could end up in an even bigger mess than we're in already.' His gaze raked over her. 'But I don't want to sleep alone tonight,' he went on in a thick voice.

'Then don't,' she said simply.

She sensed, rather than saw, the shudder that ran through him.

'You're sure you know what you're saying?' he questioned her a little roughly.

'I might be half-asleep, but I'm not rambling,' she assured him softly.

'I hope not! And I don't want you to forget it this time, either,' Lewis instructed in a suddenly hard tone. 'I want you to remember every single second of it.'

That wouldn't be difficult. Lorel had the feeling that it was going to be emblazoned on her memory for the rest of her life.

Lewis didn't waste any time. His hands were already moving over her compulsively, removing the rest of her clothes while he murmured softly with pleasure at the treasures he was uncovering. His movements seemed to Lorel to be both familiar and yet, at the same time, completely new to her. It was a fascinating combination of sensations, which she found curiously arousing.

She undid the buttons on his shirt as surely as if she had done it a dozen—a hundred—times before. Then she laid her palms flat against the hard warmth of his chest, feeling the contraction of his muscles as he instantly responded.

'Do you remember how much I enjoyed it when you touched me?' he murmured huskily.

No, she didn't remember, but it didn't matter. It was almost better like this, discovering it all over again, giving in to the impulse to explore further until Lewis exclaimed out loud, his breath abruptly catching in his throat.

'Cut that out,' he growled with mock fierceness. 'Or this will be over in two minutes, not five!'

There was now a ragged impatience in his voice. He picked her up and tossed her lightly on to the bed, stripped off the last of his own clothes, and then slid down beside her.

His kisses were bruising this time, marking her mouth and her skin as his lips travelled over her at random. His fingers explored with equal restlessness, not caring how intimately they touched and caressed, leaving all of Lorel's nerve-ends in total disarray.

When he moved still closer, his skin felt unexpectedly silky against her own, and hot, very hot. Or was the heat coming from her own body? She didn't know; could no longer tell. Tiredness and an aching sense of pleasure spread through her in equal measure. Her limbs felt as if they were floating, her head was woolly, and yet parts of her were on fire.

She looked up at Lewis confusedly, and muttered
something incoherently under her breath. Although
he couldn't possibly have understood the words, he
seemed to know exactly what she had said.

'It's all right, sweetheart,' he murmured. 'Leave
everything to me.'

His movements were hard and sure; his hands
guided and positioned her, and then gentled when they
detected a faint flutter of nervousness. Her mind and
senses spinning, Lorel blindly followed and obeyed.

Deeper and deeper he took her, sometimes leading,
and sometimes waiting for her to catch up, his own
impatient desires held tightly in check. It was like an
intricate dance, which could only be performed perfectly when the two partners were completely in step.

Then darkness began to whirl about them; the dance
became faster and more frenzied, and Lorel heard her
own breath gasping softly in her lungs. Lewis heard
and moved again, closing the circle, and sliding his
mouth over her own to catch her stifled words of love
and delight.

Lorel dimly realised that his own needs had finally
reached the stage where they were becoming quite un-
manageable, but it didn't seem to matter. Each wave
of pleasure that lapped over her was a little fiercer
than the last, as the dance whisked her faster and faster
towards its exquisite climax, where she hovered in
suspended delight for what seemed like half a lifetime
before her sweat-soaked and pleasure-drugged body
at last drifted back to reality.

Lewis lay as still as she did, his weight crushing her,
and his heart pounding wildly against her own ribs.
At last, his heartbeat and breathing eased back to near-
normal, and he carefully shifted his weight off her.

'Still awake?' he murmured against her ear.

'I think so,' Lorel muttered. 'Although I might we
be dreaming. It's hard to tell.'

'Do you usually have dreams that interesting?' h
teased gently.

Lorel began to smile, but half-way through it turne
into a yawn.

Lewis pulled her closer, so that she was com
fortably wedged up against him. 'Go to sleep,' he o
dered softly.

Obediently, Lorel closed her eyes. In just second
she had forgotten all her problems and slid into
gentle and peaceful state of oblivion.

When she woke up again, it was morning, and sh
gradually became aware of three things.

First—and most important—Lewis was no long
sharing the bed with her. In fact, there was no sig
that he had ever been there. The pillow had been car
fully fluffed up where his dark head had dented i
and the bedclothes straightened on his side. Then sh
noticed the scrawled note on the table beside her.

She grabbed it, and hurriedly scanned the coupl
of lines it contained.

'I thought I'd better leave before Maria comes u
with your breakfast tray. I don't want her to kno
that she's totally failed in her efforts to guard yo
virtue! Lewis.'

Lorel read it through twice, oddly disappointed a
the impersonal tone of the note. No words of lov
or even affection. Even the scribbled signature ha
been added without any endearment attached to it.

She slowly swung her legs over the side of the be
and then just sat there for a few moments, still feelin
an unexpected physical tiredness, even after her nig
of very sound sleep. Then she made her second di
covery of the morning. Her missing chunk of memor

ad come back at some time during the night, while
ae had slept. The blank couple of days were now
erfectly clear in her mind—it was as if they had never
een missing. She could recall absolutely everything,
om her first meeting with Lewis on the station, to
ae moment when she had stolen his briefcase.

With a small shiver, she also remembered that first
me he had taken her to bed. It had been just as good
s it had been last night, which was perhaps why she
ad felt such a strong sense of guilt and shame after-
ards. To share all that deep intimacy with someone
ho, at the time, she hadn't even known very well—

wonder she had preferred to push it right out of
er memory! She supposed it had been her way of
retending to herself that it hadn't even happened.

But it had. And so had last night. Lorel shivered
gain, from the certainty that Lewis intended to take
aings even further.

A slight cramping pain in the pit of her stomach
rought the third revelation of the morning to her
tention. In fact, there was a familiar ache starting
p all around her lower body, and her eyes began to
egister comprehension.

A hurried trip to the bathroom confirmed her sus-
icions. Whatever had caused that hiccup in her
onthly cycle, it definitely wasn't pregnancy. The
iscovery numbed her. She hadn't realised that she
ad already begun to accept her pregnancy as a fact.
aced with the incontrovertible evidence that no baby
xisted, she felt an appalling sense of emptiness. The
erceness of her reaction stunned her. She had
xpected to feel utter relief if a pregnancy test proved
egative. Instead, she just wanted to sit down and cry
om the sheer sensation of loss.

She stayed in the bathroom for ages, trying to get herself together. It's much better this way, she argued weakly with herself. She couldn't shake off the deep sense of resentment, though, at the way her body had played such a mean trick on her.

She finally washed, and got dressed. Then she went back into the bedroom and sat by the window for a while. The city glowed in the clear morning sunshine. Venice—the magic city, she thought to herself. Well, this morning it somehow seemed rather tarnished.

Maria brought in her breakfast tray a little later, but Lorel didn't feel like eating. In fact, she wasn't sure *what* she felt like. The last twenty-four hours had been such a mixture of highs and lows that her head—and her emotions—were still whizzing round in dizzy circles.

Half an hour later, there was a light tap at the door, and this time it was Lewis who came in. Although Lorel had been expecting to see him, the actual sight of him still made her stomach flip right over.

He stood just inside the doorway, his blue gaze resting on her thoughtfully.

'Are you hiding from me?' he said at last.

'Yes,' she said, with complete honesty.

'I thought so. Want to tell me why?'

Lorel shifted position a little restlessly. There were several things she wanted to tell him, but she supposed she ought to get the most important one over with first.

'My period's started,' she said bluntly. 'I'm not pregnant. The sickness and dizziness must have been just a virus, after all.'

To her surprise, a look of acute disappointment crossed Lewis's face.

'I thought you'd be relieved,' she said slowly.

'Why did you think that?'

Lorel had the impression that the question had come at rather more harshly than he had intended. She gave a puzzled frown. She hadn't expected him to react like this.

'Well, it's a let-out for you, isn't it?' she reminded him, reluctantly putting into words what had been very obvious to her ever since her discovery this morning. 'You don't have to feel responsible for me any more. You're free of any commitments.'

Lewis came further into the room. 'Have I ever said I wanted that kind of freedom?'

'No,' she muttered. 'But——'

'But what?' he demanded, his tone still rough.

Her nerves suddenly felt very frayed. 'No man wants to be tied to someone because of an unplanned baby,' she snapped back at him. 'It's a well-known fact. I should think you're very relieved that things have turned out this way.'

'Stop assuming that you know what I'm feeling. You don't!' He ran his fingers irritably through his hair. 'Sometimes I think that you never have done,' he added, in a dark tone.

Lorel instantly bristled. 'That's hardly surprising. You never tell me!'

His blue eyes shot round to fix on her. 'What exactly do you mean by that?'

'Take last night,' she retorted, with a sudden surge of resentment. 'Did you enjoy it? Was I anything more than a couple of pleasant hours in bed? Did it *mean* anything to you?'

Lewis stared at her in sheer disbelief. 'How the hell can you think it didn't?'

'Quite easily! I'm not a mind-reader. I need to b *told* how you feel about things—about me,' she fin ished, on a rather faltering note.

Lewis came a little nearer. 'I'm not much good a putting things into words,' he growled.

'Well, you'd better try, or we're never going to ge any of this sorted out.'

'Where do you want to start?' he said, after a shor pause.

'Right at the beginning, I suppose.' Lorel lifted he head. 'Oh, there's something else you ought to know I've got my memory back.' Her eyes briefly sparkled 'Every single second of it,' she added meaningfully.

'Then you know by now that I didn't force you int bed with me on that train.'

'I think I knew it all along,' she admitted frankly 'It was just an excuse to keep you at arm's length. I was nervous about getting involved with you.'

'Am I that alarming?' he asked drily.

'No, not really. It was just me, being a coward.' Lorel suddenly grinned. 'When I first met you, I didn't think you were alarming at all. Just a mannerless pig!'

Lewis's eyebrows shot up. 'I hope you've changed your opinion of me since then.'

'Yes, I have,' she said kindly. 'There are days when I'm really quite fond of you.'

'You were more than fond of me last night,' he re- minded her.

The colour flooded into her face. 'I know,' she mumbled.

'In fact, at one point you even said that you loved me,' Lewis went on.

She looked at him guardedly. 'That might have been just a slip of the tongue.'

'It might have been,' he agreed, his gaze flicking
ver her assessingly. 'Yet I don't think that it was.'

Nervousness made her tone edgy. 'You're assuming
n awful lot!'

'Perhaps.' His blue eyes glinted. 'But I think that
'm entitled to, don't you?'

Lorel wasn't sure how to answer that, so she stayed
ilent.

'I wonder what it is about you,' he went on
ausingly, almost as if speaking to himself. 'There have
een women in my life before—a couple of the re-
ationships nearly became serious, although I found
ayself backing off at the last minute—but none of
aem were quite like you.'

'In what way?' Lorel asked curiously.

A wry smile settled around Lewis's mouth. 'In any
ay at all. Believe it or not, I don't usually take
omen to bed when I've known them for only a few
ours. Yet I could hardly keep my hands off you on
aat train. And when you hit your head and couldn't
emember any of it, I was partly furious because I
aought I'd lost the advantage that had given me, and
artly relieved, because I realised it gave me the chance
a make a fresh start with you. I thought you might
ppreciate a more conventional approach!'

Lorel remembered something else. 'I only fell and
it my head because you were chasing me,' she re-
ainded him tartly. Then she gave a rueful grimace.
This whole thing has been a big mix-up right from
ae start, hasn't it?'

Lewis looked at her steadily. 'Does that really
aatter, as long as we know where we're going from
ere?'

'I suppose not.' Then she frowned at him. 'Where
e we going?'

'How about back to England, to meet my family?'
Lewis suggested.

She blinked. 'Your family?'

'You'll like Katie, and you'll probably be charmed
by Felix, my stepbrother—although not too charmed,
I hope,' he said warningly. 'As for Rita, my stepmother——' Lewis gave a resigned shrug. 'She'll
probably drive you a little crazy, but I think you're
tough enough to cope with her.'

'Er—why should I *want* to meet them?' Lorel asked
carefully.

'Isn't that obvious?' replied Lewis, his face perfectly bland. 'It's only reasonable that they should
meet my future wife before the wedding.'

'Wedding?' Lorel repeated, parrot-like, her mind a
little too numb to find anything more intelligent to
say.

'You love me,' Lewis told her calmly. 'And I'm
damned sure I must love you, or I'd never have let
you turn my life upside-down the way you have. What
else can we do, except get married?'

Lorel was suddenly a little irritated at the way he
was railroading her into this.

'A lot of things!' she retorted. 'Anyway, I'm no
absolutely sure that I *do* love you.'

Lewis remained unruffled. 'Of course you do,' he
replied cheerfully. 'In fact, I think you fell for me the
first moment you saw me. There are a lot of people
who scoff at love at first sight, but I reckon that you
could prove them wrong.'

She glared fiercely at him. 'You are so big-headed
And wrong! I'm far too sensible to fall in love with
some stranger I met on a train.'

'Then why did you jump into bed with me?' came
Lewis's calm challenge. 'You're not the sort of gir

who's going to clamber into anyone's bed unless you've got pretty strong feelings for them.'

That effectively silenced her, because he was right. He was always right, she thought to herself a little sulkily. It was going to be quite infuriating if he kept it up right through their married life.

Married life? she repeated to herself silently. Married—to Lewis?

He stood and quietly watched her come to terms with the idea.

'We've only known each other three weeks,' she muttered at last.

'That's quite long enough for me. I know exactly what I want—all you've got to do now is to make up your mind.'

Lorel chewed her lip warily. 'There's still such a lot we don't know about each other.'

'What do you want me to do? Fill in a written questionnaire, giving all the missing details?' Lewis gave a sudden, impatient shake of his head. 'We know all we need to know, all the important things. The rest we can learn as we go along.'

He made it sound so easy, so straightforward—and so tempting!

She remembered something else. 'You were really upset when I told you there wasn't any baby, weren't you?' she said quietly.

'Yes, I was,' he admitted frankly. Then his eyes glowed. 'Although it shouldn't be too difficult to remedy the situation—if you want to.'

'Yes, I do,' she said in a soft voice.

Lewis's features relaxed. He walked slowly over to her, and then stood there, looking down at her.

'You're willing to risk it, then?'

Lorel looked directly back into his vivid blue eyes. 'I don't think it'll be such a risk.' Then she grinned. 'After all, you're a very successful businessman,' she reminded him. 'You wouldn't take on any new venture unless you were very sure it was going to succeed!'

'I've never taken on anything quite like this before,' Lewis remarked wryly. 'But I'm damned sure it's going to turn out to be the best move I've ever made in my life.'

'All right, then.' She nodded happily. 'Marriage it is.' Then she grinned again.

'What are you laughing at?' he demanded.

'You look so very pleased with yourself. Like a small boy at Christmas, who's just been given the very present that he wanted.'

Lewis's own mouth curled up at the corners. 'Perhaps that's how I feel. Except that I got to open my present last night,' he went on, in a more husky tone.

'And did you like it?' Lorel asked demurely. 'Did it live up to your expectations?'

'Yes,' he said simply. Then his eyes gleamed. 'So much so, that I'd like to play with it all over again,' he added throatily.

'That's not possible at the moment,' Lorel reminded him regretfully.

'It doesn't matter. I've already decided that, from now on, we're going to do things properly. There'll be no more games in the bedroom until *after* we're married.'

Lorel wrinkled her nose in disappointment. 'None at all?'

'Perhaps just a kiss—or maybe two,' Lewis conceded. 'So that we don't entirely forget how to go about it. But that's as far as it goes,' he went on.

ternly. 'If necessary, I'll take Maria home with us,
o act as temporary chaperon until we're married.'

Lorel looked at him mischievously. 'She hasn't done
a very good job so far,' she reminded him.

'That's because she rather misguidedly trusts me.
f I drop just one little hint about what happened last
night, she'll make sure she doesn't let you out of her
ight until we're legally married.'

'Am I really going to need that sort of close
haperoning?'

'Oh, yes,' murmured Lewis. 'You are most definitely going to need it!'

He bent his head, and his fierce kiss confirmed his
words.

A little breathless, Lorel gazed into his vivid blue
yes. 'You promised I could have two kisses,' she reminded him huskily.

Lewis gave a faint groan. 'One was difficult enough.
Two might turn out to be more than I can handle.
How much will-power do you think I've got?'

'You're quite safe,' Lorel told him. 'I can hear
Maria's footsteps coming up the stairs. I'd say we've
ot about—oh, ten seconds before she gets here.'

'Then I suppose we should make the most of them,'
Lewis murmured, and proceeded to give Lorel ten of
the most delicious seconds of her life.

Harlequin Presents

Coming Next Month

Available in April wherever paperback books are sold, or through Harlequin Reader Service:

In the U.S.
901 Fuhrmann Blvd.
P.O. Box 1397
Buffalo, N.Y 14240-1397

In Canada
P.O. Box 603
Fort Erie, Ontario
L2A 5X3

This April, don't miss Harlequin's new Award o
Excellence title from

CAROLE MORTIMER

Award of
Excellence

elusive as the unicorn

*When Eve Eden discovered that Adam
Gardener, successful art entrepreneur, was
searching for the legendary English artist, The
Unicorn, she nervously shied away. The Unicorn
true identity hit too close to home....*

*Besides, Eve was rattled by Adam's
mesmerizing presence, especially in the light
of the ridiculous coincidence of their names—
and his determination to take advantage of it
But Eve was already engaged to marry her
longtime friend, Paul.*

*Yet Eve found herself troubled by the differen
choices Adam and Paul presented. If only the
answer to her dilemma didn't keep eluding he*

HP'